MYSTERY AT MANATEE CREEK

Robert Tylander -

Kanuga. 2000

MYSTERY AT MANATEE CREEK

ROBERT TYLANDER

Pittsburgh, PA

ISBN 1-56315-204-5

Paperback Fiction
© Copyright 1999 Robert Tylander
All rights reserved
First Printing—2000
Library of Congress #98-88536

Request for information should be addressed to:

SterlingHouse Publisher, Inc.
The Sterling Building
440 Friday Road
Pittsburgh, PA 15209
www.sterlinghousepublisher.com

Cover design: AJ Rodgers - SterlingHouse Publisher
Typesetting: Venture Graphics USA

Printed in Canada

DEDICATION

To my wonderfully patient wife, Mary Merle, who has read and edited so many drafts of this novel she could recite it in her sleep.

To my high school friends and teammates, Charles Sample, Larry "Hunk" Slay and Edgar Register. Charles and Hunk are no longer with us, but they read and approved the manuscript.

ACKNOWLEDGEMENTS

Melba Bowie and Jeannie Gooch for their advice and suggestions. Ann McKinney, Paul Bockhoven and others on the staff at the Kanuga Conference. Robin Smith for his help with the cover. The late Robert Enns, former editor of The Tribune in Fort Pierce, Florida for interesting me in writing after my retirement. Cynthia Sterling, publisher, for finding some good in the original and shorter versions of this story and for "strongly encouraging" me to keep going.

CHAPTER 1

The toot-toot of the switch engine's whistle signaled its arrival as Harcord Ritchie and I hustled the last of the lumber out of the boxcar in which the temperature was about 120 degrees. Sweat was pouring down my forehead and stinging my eyes so that I could hardly see Harcord, a strong, hard-working colored man who was helping me unload the lumber into a shed adjacent to a railroad siding.

"Harcord," I said, as the switch engine noisily hitched on to the empty boxcar, "Dad has each of his sons work in the yard at least one summer so as to expose us to the lumber business. My brothers, Bill and Jeff, liked it but as for me, there must be a better way to make a living."

I have known Harcord as a good friend most of my life. His Bahamian-born mother worked for a family that lived two blocks south of us on Fort Capron's riverfront. When he was a youngster, Harcord often came to work with her, and though he was colored, he was always welcome to play with us, which was unusual in our county. My father hired Harcord when there were cars to unload. He would have liked to employ him full-time, but business was slow.

Smiling his usual good-natured smile, Harcord said, "Come on, this work won't hurt you none. It's Thursday, and your daddy shuts down at noon. Jus' think about that cool ocean water you'll be swimmin' in at the beach this after-noon."

My father was Ward Forrester, the owner of a builder's supply business in Fort Capron, San Lucia County, Florida.

My name is Scott Forrester. It was the summer of 1933 and six weeks ago I graduated from San Lucia County High School.

All the businesses in Fort Capron closed at noon on Thursday. It was recreation time in our county. Mar-Rio Golf Course and the local tennis courts were well-patronized, while other folks were gardening, boating, and fishing, and otherwise enjoying leisure time. The ocean beach was usually crowded with high school and college kids cooling off in the summer heat. After going home for lunch, I was to pick up my buddies, Charles Graham and Eddie Russell, for an afternoon at the beach.

As we parted, I said, "Hey, that was a fine job of work we did this morning. I don't look forward to unloading these freight cars, but when I must, there's nobody else I would rather have on the other end of that lumber. It was good to be with you, and tell your mother I said hello."

"So long. Enjoy the beach." I sensed some wistfulness in Harcord's voice because to my knowledge, he had never been in the ocean at our beach. He and his friends in Ruby Town had to do their swimming below a spillway in one of the drainage canals near his home. Ruby Town was the name of the section where the coloreds lived in northwestern Fort Capron.

It had always bothered me somewhat that Harcord and people like him were limited in where they could go, and what they could do. Apparently it didn't bother me much, because I never did anything about it, except I did try to be friendly to Harcord and the other coloreds. My mother, Clara Forrester, taught me not to use the word "nigger" and I never have.

I drove through town to our house on the bluff overlooking the Indian River, a wide body of saltwater lying between the mainland and a barrier island fronting the Atlantic Ocean. Most of the Fort Capron people resided within a square mile area; citrus growing, truck farming, cattle raising, and fishing provided them with their principal income.

Spanish missionaries visited this region in the sixteenth century seeking to convert the natives to Christianity. Their only success was in providing the area with geographical names. Even though it may have a few warts, all in all our small town was a good place in which to live.

Arriving home, I parked my car on the street behind our house, went in the rear entrance between the wash house and the pump house, and through the back porch to the kitchen where Mother was preparing dinner for the family, which then consisted of my parents and me. My sisters were married; Harriet lived in Marietta, Georgia, where her husband was the Ford dealer, and Mary was the wife of a local lawyer. My older brother, Bill, was in Tennessee training to be a sales representative for a major roofing company. Jeff was in Oregon learning the lumber industry literally from the ground up. He had been awarded a scholarship to Weyerhauser Lumber Institute in Portland when he graduated from high school two years ago. I will be going to the University of Florida in the fall.

After washing up, I joined the others at the table.

"How did the work go this morning?" my father asked me, knowing very well how hot it was unloading a freight car of lumber in July. He had done it himself many times in his younger days.

"Oh, it was a fun morning," I joked, "but I suggest that you and Roger arrange to have several blocks of ice installed in each boxcar before we unload it."

Roger Hoyt, Fort Capron's young mayor, owned the local ice plant across the railroad track from the lumber yard. The lumber yard, ice plant, Brackett Boat Yard, and much of the commercial fishing activity bordered Monroe Creek, which flowed into the Indian River.

"What a suggestion," Dad laughingly replied. "I'll take

that under consideration. By the way, there's an order for seventy-five sacks of cement to be delivered when we open up tomorrow morning, and you've been elected to take care of it."

"Ward, take it easy on Scott," Mother said. "You're going to wear him out. He hasn't had any time off since graduation. How much longer does he have to work before he goes up to visit Harriet?"

"Until the middle of August, which is three more weeks. As you know, he goes to freshman orientation at the University, and then to Marietta. He'll have the last ten days of August and part of September to play."

"I'm really looking forward to that trip to Marietta. But now, I'm headed for the beach," I said.

After excusing myself from the table, I went upstairs, showered, and pulled on a polo shirt and shorts over my swimming trunks.

I left the house to pick up my friends Eddie and Charles in the 1928 Ford Model-A roadster that Dad had given me during the past school year. He'd taken it in settlement of a debt from a fellow who had bought material to build a boat shed and fish-net racks on Monroe Creek.

The man was originally a fisherman from Brielle, New Jersey, and had come to Florida to make his fortune in the 1920's economic bubble known as the Florida Boom. He was one of several salesmen for the nationally advertised development in the north part of the county known as Indian River Shores, which was started in the latter days of the boom. A few lots were sold and some buildings built, including an elaborate railroad station, before the bubble finally burst in 1928. That put an end to Indian River Shores, and most of the other real estate activity in southern Florida.

The real estate salesman was stuck in San Lucia County.

He scratched out a living doing yard work and picking fruit, but decided to go back to fishing. The bill that he ran up at the lumber yard was more than his Ford was worth, but Dad accepted the car in settlement to help the man get started.

My father had suffered considerably from the economic depression that followed the end to the Florida boom, partially brought on by hurricanes in the years 1926 and 1928. Due to these disasters, what became known as the Great Depression began earlier in Florida than in other parts of the country. Things were looking better, but there had been days when my father didn't know if his business would survive. Anyway, I came off lucky in that deal, because I was one of the very few students who drove a car to school each day.

We had the Model-A painted a deep green with black fenders. A white cover on the spare wheel and tire mounted on the rear of the roadster had a green eagle in full flight painted in the center and bore the legend "Fighting Eagles," the name by which the athletic teams at San Lucia County High were known. With money I made working on weekends and after school, I added rear fender flaps, a horn that sounded a three-tone chord, and best of all, a down-draft carburetor. Mike Rosman, of Rosman's garage, assured me that the engine would run smoother and the car perform better with such a carburetor. I paid the twenty dollars he asked for the installation, but I couldn't see that it made much difference in the way the car operated. Anyway, there was some satisfaction in smugly telling anyone who asked that my car had a downdraft carburetor.

Charles was with Eddie at Stoddard's filling station and restaurant where Eddie worked. When I drove up, he climbed into the car without bothering to open the door, the folding top being down. Eddie climbed into the rumble seat in back, and we were off to the beach. The Indian River, which extended for more than a hundred miles along Florida's east coast, was not really a river. It probably should have been classified as a lagoon. Opposite Fort Capron, the water was one to two miles wide, bridged at one of its narrower points by a causeway. We crossed to Hutchinson Island and parked the car in front of a two-story building constructed during the boom days. On the first floor was a food concession area with booths, tables for ping-pong and pool, a small dance floor, and dressing areas with lockers in the rear. Upstairs was a hall large enough for community celebrations and special dance events. This place was known as the Beach Casino.

The younger kids of Fort Capron who had arrived earlier would have spent most of the day alternating between dips in the ocean and hanging out in the casino.

When we walked into the casino, a table of junior high-aged girls interrupted their soda-sipping with a flurry of giggles. I went outside to greet friends who were beginning to gather for the afternoon while Eddie and Charles went to the locker room to put on their bathing trunks. They came down to the beach where I was waiting and we plunged into the small ocean rollers breaking on the shore and swam out over a coral reef.

Taking deep breaths, we dove down to watch schools of colorful fish, frightened by our presence, darting in and out of coralline hideouts. We dove at the reef for a while before swimming an easy Australian crawl a mile down the beach to where the remains of a public pavilion lay half buried in the sand. The pavilion had been there and used as the beach gathering place before the causeway bridge was built. In those days, people came to the beach by ferry from a dock in Fort Capron.

We finished our swim, waded ashore and stretched out on the roof of the old building, watching pelicans plummet down from the sky, ending in a splash as the big birds scooped up their dinner. We could see the unfortunate fish still flapping inside the pelicans' bills as they flew away to nests in the mangroves on the western shore of the island.

Charles and Eddie searched for shells along the beach. I stayed lounging on the old roof, and before long, the morning's work, the warm sun, and the sound of the waves washing up on the shore had me enjoying a nap. Eddie shook me awake and said, "Come on, buddy, you've been sleeping long enough. Let's get back to where the action is."

The receding tide made walking easy on the hard packed sand. Also it left a wide beach, and as we returned, we could see a softball game underway. Many more of the young people had come, and a few girls were playing in the game with the boys. There were no teams; the participants were playing individually in a game of work-up. Players were at every position, and they would advance when a batter or a runner made an out. The goal was to work your way up to be a batter. An exception to the rule was that an outfielder who caught a fly ball could immediately go to bat, and did not have to work his or her way up.

As latecomers, we had to take our places in the outfield. At bat was Marvin Jackson, one of our best high school baseball players. I knew he could hit a ball a mile, even though he was batting left-handed, rather than right-handed as he normally would. The girls insisted that the boy batters switch-hit as a handicap. It was not much of a handicap for Marvin. I positioned myself so far out in right field that I was standing in the ocean.

Taunting Marvin, I yelled at him, "Come on, you can't hit the broad side of a barn. Let's see if you can get one this far. I don't think you can do it." Sure enough, he rose to the bait, took a mighty swing and hit a long fly right to me, and I caught it. That entitled me to be the next batter.

When I got to bat, Charles's cousin Lil Graham was

pitching. Good athlete that she was, I expected her to try to throw a fast one by me. Instead, she tossed a high looping soft pitch right across the plate. I took a hefty swing, and fell down, missing the ball. Everybody got a big laugh out of that.

"Aw, don't throw me those sissy pitches. Burn it in here."

Lil did throw a faster one, and I was lucky enough to hit it over Charles playing second base, and the ball rolled down the beach where Eddie fielded it. As I was rounding first base, I saw a girl playing third, and figured I could make a triple easy. I waved at Charles as I went by second base, but he was busy waiting for the ball Eddie was throwing to him. As I was heading for third, Charles caught the ball, and turned and fired it to the girl on third. I tried a hook slide into the bag, but that girl took the throw from Charles and in one sweeping motion she put a tag on me that I could feel down to the bone. Eddie and Charles led the cheer that went up from the rest of the players who were happy to see me humiliated.

Getting up slowly and rubbing my shin where this girl, whom I didn't recognize, had tagged me, I said, "Hey. You play rough. Don't you know that girls aren't supposed to be that good?"

"No, I don't know that, and maybe hereafter you won't try to stretch a lucky double into a triple," she replied. Wiping the sand from my eyes, I got my first good look at my tormentor, good-looking she was. I introduced myself and that is how it all started.

CHAPTER 2

"My name is Scott Forrester, but you can call me Scotty. Everybody else does, except my mother," I said to the prettiest third baseman I had ever seen. "What's yours, and where did you come from?" I asked.

"My name is Sally Graham, and I came from Atlanta to visit my cousin Lil. And who are you, other than a boy that everyone but your mother calls Scotty?" she replied.

I started to tell her, but by then Lil and Charles had come over to celebrate my mortifying out, which had brought the game to an end. Giving Sally a big hug, Charles said, "Way to go, Sally. You really nailed him. Scotty, I forgot to tell you that Lil has company from Atlanta. Sally's a cousin, also."

"Then why is she from Atlanta?" I asked. "All you Grahams are supposed to be from Mecklenburg County in North Carolina." Three Graham brothers, Andrew, Harold and John, came to San Lucia County from North Carolina before the turn of the century. They and their wives and children were among San Lucia County's early settlers, and the families continue to be important contributors to the community.

"There was another brother, Frank. He's Sally's daddy, who stayed in North Carolina to look after the family farm, but eventually the farm was sold and he moved to Atlanta," Charles explained.

Lil said that Sally, a recent graduate of Atlanta High, had won the Atlanta high school girls' tennis championship that year. After having seen her handle the glove in the softball game this came as no surprise to me because it was easy to see that she was a good athlete.

Charles suggested that we take a dip to cool off. With her hazel eyes shining in her smiling face, Sally tucked her dark brunette hair into a white bathing cap and ran for the ocean with me right behind her. Eddie joined us with Nell Stone, also from Georgia, who was visiting a sister in Fort Capron for the summer. Lil had gone to the casino to watch her steady boyfriend, Randy Howell, play ping-pong.

After a refreshing swim, Charles took off jogging down the beach. Eddie, Nell, Sally, and I stretched out on beach towels to bake our skins to a toasty brown in the hot Florida sun. I managed to maneuver a position alongside Sally.

The events of the past few years had tested the character of our generation. As small children, most of us saw our families enjoy seemingly never-ending prosperity in the Florida boom days, only to have to adjust to hard economic times after the end of the boom, two devastating hurricanes, the stock market crash in 1929, and subsequent bank closings.

My father was on the board of directors of a bank that had failed. As required by law, he not only lost his investment in the bank as well as the funds he had on deposit, but was also liable to the depositors for an amount equal to his investment. Were it not for the shame, it would have been financially easier on him and his family if he had taken bankruptcy. But because of his pride and his obligation to the depositors, he did not consider bankruptcy to be an option. Fortunately, his reputation was such that his suppliers were generous in extending credit so that he could keep his business operating.

Many of the people in the county had been out of work. Some of the mothers of our friends took work heading shrimp in a shrimp-packing plant. Eddie's father, who once was an active businessman, was working as a night watchman in a citrus packinghouse. Charles's mother and father had died, and he lived sometimes with his sister, whose husband was trying to sell insurance, and sometimes with his uncle in a citrus grove west of town. There was no way Eddie could go to college, but Charles had a track scholarship to Davidson College in North Carolina. Charles held the Florida high school pole-vaulting record.

Perhaps because it began here earlier, a feeling existed in this part of Florida that the depression was beginning to run its course, and our people were shaking off the despair. The youth of our generation had weathered the worst and there was hope on the horizon for better days.

I finally realized that I was rambling on about the way things were in Florida during which Sally had been mostly quiet, with only an occasional comment. Thinking that it was about time to change the subject and get to know this very attractive girl better, I began brilliantly by saying, "How are things in Atlanta?"

"Now, Scott," she said, "and I choose to call you Scott, do you really want to know how things are in Atlanta, or is that just your way of starting a conversation?"

"Well, it was the only thing that came to mind. I have a sister who lives in Marietta, and will be visiting her next month. While I'm there I expect to go to some places in Atlanta, but if you would prefer, I'll talk about myself and Florida."

"I'm sorry—that wasn't very nice of me. Marietta's a fine historical town, and I would be glad to tell you about Atlanta. But, as a matter of fact, I have been listening with interest about the Sunshine State, and I would like to learn more," Sally replied. "I heard that you were in Miami in February and saw President Roosevelt's near-assassination."

"How did you hear that?" I asked.

"Lil told me before I even met you today. You're famous around here, you know."

"I'm not famous," I said. "I just happened to be with my

father on a business trip in Miami. Roosevelt was on a pre-inauguration visit and appearing at a rally in Bayfront Park with Anton Cermak, the mayor of Chicago. Dad and I decided to go to see the president-elect, arriving early to get a good seat among the benches close to the podium. Proceedings were just beginning, when a guy ran around from the back of the dignitaries' stage, and yelled, 'People are starving,' and fired a gun in the podium's direction. The bullet missed Roosevelt, but hit Mayor Cermak. Before a second shot could be fired, the assassin was overwhelmed by Miami policemen."

"What did you do?" Sally asked.

"When the man was running toward the stage and yelling, Dad and I rose up to get a better look, but when I saw him fire the gun, I dove down behind the bench in front of us. In the pandemonium, I assumed that our soon-to-be president was shot, but upon rising from the ground, I saw Roosevelt still sitting on the stage surrounded by secret service men, while Cermak was slumped down in his chair being attended to by what appeared to be a doctor. Of course, we learned later that Cermak died."

"Why would anyone want to do such a thing?"

"Like the man said, 'people are starving'. Desperate times make desperate men. The poor guy didn't help things much. He's to be executed for his crime."

"Well, compared to Georgia, so much seems to be happening in Florida. You all have had this rum-running thing going on for years. We read about it in the papers all the time."

"When liquor became illegal in the United States, people were going to get their booze somehow," I replied, turning over to tan my back and get a better look at Sally. "Florida's nearness to the British Bahamas made it easy to smuggle the stuff in here. Once the booze arrives, the local law enforcement officers don't do much as they're often bought off,

knowing that most people don't care whether or not the bootlegging is stopped. It is still going on even though the
Prohibition Amendment will probably be repealed before the
end of the year."

"Folks have been making moonshine whiskey in stills in
the Georgia mountains for years," Sally said. "It first started
in the Appalachians a long time ago when the government
began taxing the alcohol in whiskey made from corn. They
call it 'moonshine' because it's usually made at night so that
revenue agents can't see the smoke rising from the fire while
the batch is cooking."

Looking at Sally I found it difficult to concentrate on
what I was saying but I continued anyway, "I understand that
moonshine is the whiskey of choice in Florida's panhandle
area, but around here the real McCoy is easy to get. The
British-made whiskey is referred to by the name of a famous
bootlegger."

"Don't you have law enforcement people who even try to
stop it?" Sally asked.

"We do have a sheriff who makes an appearance of
enforcing the law, but he doesn't work very hard at it. Many
of our people are in favor of prohibition and don't want to see
it repealed, especially the church people. When Florida voted
on the repeal, it was funny to see the church people and the
bootleggers on the same side. Neither group favored repeal.
Repeal will put the bootleggers out of business."

"How are politics around here?" Sally was an intelligent
girl, surprisingly interested in the area.

"Most folks are Democrats. A few are Republicans. In the
elections, party doesn't matter much. Folks vote on the candi-
date, or on the issue. We had an upset in the last election when
a new young lawyer, Paul Cochrane, was elected state attorney over the incumbent who was supported by our sheriff, the
power in politics around here for a long time. Our young

mayor was elected at the same time."

Our conversation was interrupted when Eddie was aroused from a short nap he was taking by Nell's shoving him and saying, "Hey, you bum, wake up! You're no company."

To which Eddie drowsily replied, "For crying out loud, a guy can't get any rest around here;" whereupon, Nell slugged him with a boat cushion she had been using as a pillow.

"Well, you have to help me listen to this boring conversation. Sally and Scotty are brainy types that you might learn something from," Nell said to Eddie.

"I have already learned from Miss Gruber that a preposition is something that you should not end a sentence with," said Eddie. Miss Gruber was our English teacher in high school.

Coming from the casino with Randy, Lil approached and said, "Come on, Sally, it's time for us to go home. Mother is having an early supper so Daddy can get to the theater. There's going to be a big crowd, inside and outside. The Bank Night jackpot is up to $350." Lil's father, Harold Graham, was manager of the Sunshine Theater.

Lil was referring to the popular lottery drawing that was held every Thursday night at the theater following the showing of the feature film. Bank Night was a gimmick used by movie houses to increase patronage. Management started the pot with $50 which was given to a person present, whose name was drawn from the names of persons who had previously registered. If the person whose name was drawn was not present, $50 was added to the pot each week until the jackpot was won by some lucky person who was present.

A substantial part of the town's population had registered and most wanted to be on hand for the event. Even though the theater has nearly a thousand seats, it could not hold them all. Mr. Graham provided coverage of the drawing over a sound system with loudspeakers outside, and recognized people as being present if they were within hearing distance of the speakers.

Going to Bank Night was the highlight of the week for many people of the community. It was inexpensive, and the crowd outside enjoyed the social contact with their friends while waiting for the feature to end inside. Furthermore, one just might win the jackpot—a sizeable stroke of good fortune in the days of money shortage.

"If you all are going to be there," Lil said, "meet us at the side door, and we can go up to Daddy's viewing box, next to the projection room."

"I'll be there for sure," I quickly said. It occurred to me that this would be an opportunity to see more of Sally. After our initial and unusual introduction, we seemed to be getting along very well.

Charles came jogging up from his run down the beach. We picked up our blankets and other paraphernalia and prepared to depart. I told Sally that I would like to see her that night; sort of asking for a date.

Sally agreed and said, "I'm looking forward to the movie. The feature is 'Morning Glory' starring that new young actress, Katharine Hepburn. She won the Academy Award this year for her performance in the movie."

We said our good-byes and Sally left with Lil and Nell in Randy's car. I waited while Eddie and Charles went in the casino and changed into their regular clothes.

On the way home Eddie said that he had promised to take his mother to Bank Night that night. They would mingle with the crowd rather than go to see the movie inside. This was a pleasant diversion for her. She did not go out much at night because of Mr. Russell's job at the packing house.

"Scotty, it looks like you have a date with Sally. We know Randy will be with Lil. So, I don't reckon I'll horn in on your party. I'll just join the crowd out in front," Charles said. I dropped Eddie and Charles off at Eddie's house, and drove on home for supper.

Randy and I were there when Lil and Sally arrived at the foot of the back stairs leading up to a landing outside a door into the balcony and projection room area of the Sunshine Theater. We ascended the long flight of stairs, passed a ticket seller's booth, and made our way along the rear of the balcony to Mr. Graham's viewing room. I stopped long enough to say hello to Harcord Ritchie, who was sitting with some of his colored friends two rows below us. The colored people were not permitted to sit on the main floor of the theater. They were required to enter by a side door and sit in the balcony.

Harcord asked, "How were things at the beach today?"

"Better than I could have hoped for," I said, nodding toward Sally.

I called Sally over and introduced her to Harcord. He removed his hat, and holding it in his hand, said, "Mighty pleased to meet you, Miss Graham." Sally acknowledged his polite greeting, and we went on into the viewing room.

The viewing room was furnished with comfortable chairs, and a cold drink machine. It was usually occupied by special friends of Sally's Uncle Harold for business and social reasons. We were guests this evening because of Sally.

"You sure were nice to that colored boy," Sally said to me. "We don't see that kind of friendliness much in Atlanta."

"We've been friends for years and Harcord is one of the most honest, hard-working persons I know."

"I understand," she said, "but that just doesn't happen often up home."

The houselights lowered and the show started with a Krazy Kat cartoon, followed by a comedy with several police-men riding on the running boards of cars, shouting and waving at whomever they were chasing.

I could see why Katharine Hepburn had won an Academy

Award for her role in "Morning Glory": she was lovely, funny, and winsome. As we sat in the dark, I found Sally's hand. It was soft and warm. At first she seemed hesitant, but her clasp was noticeably firmer in the romantic scenes.

Mr. Graham left the viewing room, and shortly thereafter the movie ended. The overhead lights came on as an attendant rolled out onto the theater stage a large round horizontally-mounted basket full of cards, and set up a microphone alongside. Mr. Graham strode on to the stage accompanied by Martha Windom, Bank Night's Girl of the Week, a local secretary selected by a Chamber of Commerce committee.

After blowing into the microphone to check the sound system Mr. Graham made a welcoming speech and introduced Martha. He directed the attendant to vigorously revolve the basket which was nearly full of Bank Night entries.

Tense excitement permeated the theater, as Martha, standing on a step-stool and blindfolded, reached deep down into the mass of cards and pulled one out. Her blindfold was removed, and without looking at the card, she walked to the microphone. She then held up the card and read from it the name of Anna Russell.

Groans and cheers sounded from the audience, and I yelled, "That's Eddie's mother!" Bedlam broke loose in the viewing room. We were all so glad for her, it was as if we had won the $350 ourselves. It meant much to me because I knew the help that the money would be in the Russell household.

Eddie came in the theater from the outside with his mother in hand and right behind them was Charles whooping and hollering. Martha assisted Mrs. Russell up the stairs onto the stage. Mr. Graham presented the winner to the audience, and told her the check would be waiting at the bank in the morning. He asked her if she would care to say what she would do with the money.

With a choke in her voice and eyes glistening, Anna

Russell first thanked God then Martha for pulling her card and said, "This means that my son, Eddie, can go to college after all."

The audience cheered. Eddie was a popular young man in our town, with lots of potential. As they left the stage, we hurried out of the viewing room and down the stairs to the soda shop next to the theater lobby. We found Mrs. Russell sitting happily at a table accepting congratulations from her many friends. Eddie was offering to buy sodas for everyone. Eventually, the crowd thinned out and Eddie and Charles took Eddie's excited mother home. They were planning to stop by the packinghouse and give Mr. Russell the good news.

We found Mr. Graham and thanked him for his hospitality. Lil's mother was with him. Lil was leaving with Randy, and, without saying anything to Sally, I asked permission to take Sally home. Mrs. Graham agreed, if we promised to not stay out too late. I told Randy that we would meet them at Deckers' Drive-in.

Sally and I went to my car parked down by the Fort Capron Hotel, which was located on the riverfront a block east of the theater. It was a pretty night, so I folded the top back on the roadster. We got in and drove off for Deckers'.

"I noticed that you asked for Aunt Mamie's permission to take me home, but not mine," Sally observed.

"Oh, gosh. I guess I didn't. I'm sorry, but it just seemed so natural, like we go well together."

"Well, maybe it did, but you don't know anything about me, and how I might feel about it."

That made me wonder, but about what, I was not sure.

On the way to Deckers' with the wind blowing her hair, Sally asked, "How can the amount of money that Eddie's mother won make it possible for Eddie to go to college?"

"To enroll in the University of Florida at Gainesville, all that's required is a diploma from a Florida high school and

$35 for the registration fee. The necessary books cost maybe $25, and one needs about $35 dollars a month for room and board, on campus or off. Any additional cost depends on the lifestyle one chooses. Knowing Eddie, he'll probably get some kind of part-time job. Three hundred fifty dollars will get Eddie well under way toward a college education," I replied.

"What a wonderful opportunity," Sally said. "I hope he takes advantage of it. I won't be going to college. My father works at the Carnegie Library, which, due to the depression, has had funding problems. He's taken a sizeable cut in salary and we just can't afford it. I lost a year in school when we moved to Atlanta and I'm a little older than I otherwise would be as a graduate. There's a situation in Atlanta that might determine the road my life takes in the not too distant future. But, I'm very happy for Eddie, and you also, of course."

Nearly all of the drive-in slots serviced by the carhops at Deckers' were taken by folks who had been part of the crowd at Bank Night. We parked in the adjacent parking lot. I wanted us to go inside to get some of the chocolate ice cream from Alfred's Dairy in West Palm Beach. For a dime, Mr. and Mrs. Decker served the deliciously rich ice cream dipped from a metal container and piled so high into a half-pint box that the lid wouldn't close. We got ours from the walk-up counter where Ruth Decker took care of us. She greeted Sally warmly after I introduced her. We found an unoccupied table and enjoyed what Sally admitted was ice cream as good as any she had ever tasted.

The place was noisy with the excitement of the evening, but it erupted when Eddie and Charles came in with Nell. "Three cheers for Russell," someone yelled. The crowd responded as the newcomers joined us at our table.

After things settled down a bit, I asked Eddie, "Are you going to take advantage of your mother's offer?"

"I don't know. This has all happened so fast, I haven't had time to think about it. Mom is serious, but I know how hard things are for her now, and she really needs my help at home."

"Isn't that your mother's decision to make?" Sally said. "Apparently, she wants a chance for you to go to college more than anything in her life right now. You aren't going to deprive her of that, are you?"

Sally seemed intent on having Eddie seize this opportunity. It was as if she had been in a similar situation, and taken a different course.

"Well, I'm beginning to realize that this will be the most important decision I've ever made. There's a lot of checking to do. I wouldn't take all of the money Mom won. Maybe I'll accept some of it, get a job in Gainesville, and try to make it through the first year. This will be a sacrifice for my folks, so if I start, I must graduate," Eddie said. "But, for now, let's just have a good time."

The girl carhops had been busy coming and going between the service counter and the cars outside. Their dexterity with the filled trays was remarkable, surpassed only by their good nature. The nation was suffering a lot of sadness and despair, but Deckers' Drive-in in Fort Capron, Florida, was a happy place to be that night.

Before going to the Grahams', Sally and I drove over the causeway to the beach, where we parked and listened to the music of Guy Lombardo and his Royal Canadians. His was said to be the sweetest music this side of heaven, and hearing it in the moonlight with a pretty girl beside me, it was. With my arm aound her shoulders, we turned to each other and talked quietly. Sally agreed to go with me to the weekly Saturday Summer Night's Dance in the Terrace Room of the Fort Capron Hotel.

As promised, we didn't stay out late. Sally accepted a kiss on the cheek as we said goodnight at the Grahams' door.

(HAPTER 3

Friday was a busy day at work, beginning with the cement delivery to a home under construction, one of the few begun in recent months. Lifting bags of cement was best done in the cooler part of the day, so I got an early start. Even so, most of the morning was consumed in the delivery. Upon returning to the yard, I was busy selling paint and other do-it-yourself supplies to customers planning to do small jobs around their homes over the weekend.

In a small town like ours there were few strangers. The friendly banter in the paint store centered around the event of the night before. Everybody was happy for the Russells.

Charles came by and discussed the planned family gathering that night at his Uncle Andrew's place in the community called Five Mile. It was a closed affair with about thirty of the Graham family scheduled to be there. For this reason, I would not be seeing Sally until Saturday night. I told Charles that my dad and I were planning to fish in front of our house in the evening.

The sun was setting behind us when Dad and I went with our fishing gear out on our dock after supper. A soft ocean breeze wafted in from the southeast and the moon shone brightly about three hours up in the sky. This night was created just for fishing off the end of the dock that extended out into the Indian River.

We fished for trout and snook with hand lines, throwing weighted rigs out into the water using shiners for bait. There was much to be said for this fishing method. After the rigs were heaved out into the water, we tied a bit of paper to the lines and fastened them lightly in a crack in the edge of the dock leaving slack back to where the line was secured. We then paid them no attention until and unless a fish hit a bait and pulled a paper off of the dock. In the interim, we sat in deck chairs and talked and quietly enjoyed the serenity.

My father was so occupied with his business and church and community activities that fishing together was about the only time we got to talk. That night the subject of our conversation turned to college and career.

"Working this summer and in the past has convinced me that the lumber and hardware business is not my cup of tea," I said.

"That's all right," Dad replied as he settled back in his deck chair, applying a match to and drawing on his favorite pipe. Between puffs, he said, "There is no reason why it should be. I have always wanted you boys to find your own way in life. You've mentioned a few vocations that interested you. Is there any one that you have settled on as you prepare to enter college?"

"When I got further along in school, I tried to imagine what would feel right. I enjoyed writing for the high school newspaper, so I am considering journalism."

Our discussion was interrupted when one of the papers was snatched from the edge of the dock and I landed a trout. While I was pulling it in , one of the other lines was hit, and my father landed another trout.

In a lull in the activity, Dad continued our conversation saying, "Journalism is a fine profession, son, and you would probably be good at it. I was impressed with some of the work you did this year in school."

"Well, I want to be in a job where I can contribute something. I know that times have been tough, but you told me that things are picking up in Florida now. I want to be an active part of what's in store for us in the future. I've about come to the conclusion that I want to be a journalist, maybe even an editor some day."

Dad sat back in his chair and, with his pipe in hand, said, "You must remember that in almost everything an editor writes, there's a contrary opinion. If he makes a point, somebody disagrees. If he finds a flaw in a popular project, people are upset. A good reporter writes the truth as he knows it to be. Often it is against something or someone. As a result, not everyone likes all journalists, be they reporters or editors. But an ethical journalist is respected, and respect is what counts."

That was the end of our serious conversation as we got involved in some serious fishing. After a while we had four trout in the three-pound range, and a lunker snook that was so big I had to put on gloves to haul it in.

There was a little more talk about college finances. My father said, "I can send you fifty dollars a month even considering the state of the economy. I hope you never have to go through anything like we have the past few years, but I have been lucky, I guess, when compared to many of our friends."

One of the lines whizzed out off the dock, and when it tightened, we knew we had something really big. Breaking from the surface of the water and soaring into the air was a tarpon with the moon reflecting off its shining scales. After the silver king splashed back into the water, it was too much for our rig, breaking the line which didn't disappoint us. The hour was growing late; it was time to gather up our things, return to the house, and retire for the night.

CHAPTER 4

Saturday, Randy Howell came into the store to buy varnish for the Snipe sailboat he was finishing in Brackett's Boat Yard. The boat was a product of the manual training shop at school, built with the advice and assistance of Tom Brackett acting as a volunteer instructor.

Knowing that Sally and I were going to the Saturday dance, Randy suggested that we double-date. I readily agreed and offered to use my car and pick him up at eight.

Overlooking the Indian River, the Terrace Room, with its wide casement windows, was open to the moonlit summer evening when Sally, Lil, Randy, and I parked alongside the hotel. The music had begun at 8:30, and we were a little late arriving. The swinging sound of the Ralph Hanson Five was coming from the hotel.

"Let's go, Randy, they are playing our song," Lil said as she hurried him through the door and on to the dance floor while the band was playing "You're Getting To Be a Habit With Me."

Sally and I followed them into the Terrace Room, which was furnished with tables and chairs, but few people were sitting in them. Almost everyone in the room was out on the floor dancing, except for some boys standing around deciding which girl to dance with next. Lil and Randy had lost no time in joining the others doing the fox-trot to the rhythm of their song, which finished as Sally and I reached the dance floor. While the band was arranging to play the next number, we didn't look for a seat; we joined the other couples promenading around the room.

"What a good band that is," Sally said. "Who are they?"

"They're all local. Ralph Hanson at the piano has been playing dance music since he was a kid. He has done some composing and is trying to put a big band together. The drummer gives lessons on the trombone and drums. He's playing the drums, because the trombonist Tom Brackett is good even though he is a boat-builder, not a trained musician. The boys on trumpet and sax play in the school orchestra."

The music resumed with the band playing the sweet strains of "Night and Day." For the first time, Sally was dancing in my arms effortlessly following my every move. Other girls said that my dancing wasn't bad, but with Sally I felt like Fred Astaire. I wasn't surprised when before long I felt a tap on my left shoulder as a voice said, "May I?" It was Charles Graham breaking in on us. "I want to dance with my cousin."

"Well, since it's you, I guess it's okay," I said as I reluctantly let her go. As they danced away, I went looking for Lil. She wasn't dancing with Randy. Popular as she was, boys had broken in on her already; I was next in line.

Dances were the principal summer activity of the young people of Fort Capron. Some boys came without dates; they were referred to as "stags". Unfortunately for those not asked, no girl would think of coming without a date. The musicians liked to play the summer dances because the music was appreciated by the dancers as they moved in and out around the floor.

When the band struck up the lightly swinging tune, "I May Be Wrong, But I Think You're Wonderful," we danced the lindy hop. The boys turned their partners to the side, and brought them back in their arms for a few steps. Then the girls swung out and twirled around as the boys passed them behind their backs, all without missing a beat of the rhythmic music.

Of course, some of the boys danced with more energy than talent. One of our friends, Archie McCready, usually came stag. He had some difficulty getting a date strong enough to dance with him for any length of time. Archie had a pump-handle style. He danced with his left arm extended, and proceeded to sway from side to side, pumping his extended arm and his partner's up and down. A girl dancing with Archie usually was looking over his shoulder at any boy not dancing, her eyes pleading with him to break.

Eventually, I was again dancing with Sally. She said how well she thought most of the Fort Capron boys danced. I told her that social dancing had grown to be important in the lives of this community through the years, but that our style was limited to the dancing she saw that night. It reminded me of a story her cousin, Charles, had told me of an experience he had recently at the Coral Gables Country Club in Miami.

Charles had been invited to a party for incoming freshmen sponsored by the Davidson alumni in South Florida. Arrangements were made for some of the local girls to be there to entertain the boys. Charles was dancing with a pretty thing who was doing her best to see that he had a good time. He noticed that the beat of the music was a little unusual, but he told me he thought it was some kind of waltz. When the music stopped, the young lady looked up at him, and batting her eyes, said "Oh, Charles, you tango divinely." If Charles was doing the tango, it was news to him.

At 10:30, the band took a half-hour intermission. During the break, we went to Deckers' for a hamburger. Many others did the same. A few went to the beach to neck and didn't come back to the dance. Most of the crowd returned, however, and the music got even livelier until the last dance when the band played the traditional "Goodnight Sweetheart." Those of us with dates danced the entire number with the girl we brought without fear of interruption from a breaker. It was the custom.

Sally and I held one another closely, nearly cheek to cheek, since she was almost as tall as I was. Oblivious to the other couples, I closed my eyes as we floated over the floor, knowing that this was a moment to be treasured among my memories. I felt as if I were falling in love.

Midnight came, the summer dance for that Saturday night was over, and it was time to head for home. Before leaving, we walked out on the hotel's dock and soaked up some moonglow. Lil and Randy sang in a group at school, and I was a glee club type. Sally joined right in as we harmonized to old songs like "Sailing Along on a Moonlight Bay," and new ones such as "It's Only a Paper Moon." It was another magic moment with Sally.

Out in the river, I saw a boat pass by and turn into Monroe Creek. As I thought about it later, the boat seemed to be riding somewhat low in the water.

We took the girls home at 12:30. Harold Graham is somewhat strict on the hours Lil keeps, as she is a bit younger than the rest of us. We lingered in the car outside the house as long as we prudently could, but when the front porch light flashed, we knew it was time to go in.

I didn't see Sally on Sunday. Her Uncle Harold had yet another brother, George, who had settled near Fort Lauderdale. George's family had not seen Sally for several years. After church, Mr. and Mrs. Graham and Lil took Sally to visit Uncle George.

At the dance on Saturday, Sally had told me of the times she had sailed with her folks on a lake near Atlanta, so I asked her to go with me on a moonlight sail Monday night. Even though she was an experienced sailor, once again she seemed to give the invitation some serious thought before agreeing to go, provided she had Mrs. Graham's approval.

The brilliant moon was climbing rapidly above the silhouetted trees on Hutchinson Island as we sailed through the silvery path reflecting on the river. Sally hiked out to windward, exuberantly shaking away the spray splashing her face as the bow of my sailboat, Lively Lady, with the lee rail awash sliced through the shimmering waves in the freshening summer breeze.

Nearing the island opposite the old ferry landing, I tacked over, and sailed south toward Manatee Creek, our destination down the river. Phosphorescent streaks glowed in the water as frightened fish fled away from our fast moving boat. Animal sounds and bird cries came from the nearby shore. After a beautiful trip, we arrived at the marker opposite the mouth of the creek, rounded up into the wind, dropped the sails, and glided partway into the channel meandering through the island. I rudder-sculled Lively Lady to an opening in the bordering mangroves where we waded ashore through the dense roots of the tropical trees and made our way a short distance to a grassy dune on the beach.

The ocean, bathed in bright moonlight, was edged by wavelets seemingly undecided as to whether to approach the land or to retreat. Entranced by the breath-taking beauty of the night, hand in hand we waded into the water. With the waves lapping around our knees, I turned Sally to me, and tilting her smiling face to mine, I gently kissed her soft lips. Sally responded warmly, moving into my arms. Even though four days before neither of us knew the other existed, we appeared to be falling in love. I know that I was.

The wondrous magic of the moment dissolved as I heard a voice shout, "Slow down! You're coming in too fast!"

"Turn that light the other way, it's blinding me," came the reply. Startled, Sally looked up at me inquiringly.

"You're coming in okay, now," the original voice said. "Did you drop off a stern anchor? We don't want to get stuck on this beach."

"Yeah, we did, we're paying it out now."

"You're coming in too fast, and too close. Hold that

line!" the voice from the beach yelled.

"What is all that shouting?" Sally asked.

Hearing more conversation I looked south from where the voices were coming and saw a light shining on a boat approaching the shore. "A boat is approaching the beach where some guys with a floodlight are guiding it in," I said as Sally moved out of my arms. We quietly waded from the ocean.

Lowering my voice, I said, "Let's sneak down that way staying close to the dune, and take a look. I think I know the answer, but I want to be sure."

"What do you think it is?"

"My guess is that bootleggers are smuggling whiskey in from the Bahamas. No roads are on the island, so the people on the beach must have come on the river. When we arrived, they were waiting for the delivery, but quiet as we were they did not hear us. We were lucky, because bootleggers don't like witnesses."

As we crept nearer, Sally whispered, "This is exciting. I've heard about bootleggers, but I never thought I would see any."

When the boat grounded lightly at the bow, and the forward hatch was opened, I said, "They're bootleggers, for sure. Cases are being passed to the men on the shore. I can just barely see the outline of the boat, and for some reason, it looks familiar. We've seen all we need to see. We better get going," I said softly.

"Let's not leave yet," Sally said. "If we get closer, maybe we can see who they are."

"Okay. But if we're spotted, we could be in for big trouble."

By crawling on the dune through the tall sea oats, we managed to get within two hundred feet of the bootleggers. We dared not raise our heads to look, but could hear what was being spoken.

"For the chances, I'm taking", one man said, "I'm not getting enough out of it. If I don't get a bigger cut, I may do something about it."

"Don't talk to me," another replied, "talk to the man on the boat."

"I will. I'm going aboard."

"Sally, really, we're leaving. I'll report this to the sheriff in the morning," I whispered.

Sally and I quietly returned to the creek, boarded Lively Lady, and silently paddled to the river. I raised the sails, and set a course for home. As Sally snuggled alongside me on the cockpit seat, I said, "Now, where were we?"

The land having cooled, a nice breeze was blowing from the mainland shore. With no more incidents, we soon arrived at our dock, secured the boat, and I took Sally to the Grahams' house. It was rather late, and no one was up.

When I kissed her goodnight and thanked her for the lovely evening, Sally said, "Yes, it was a lovely evening, but it was exciting, too. I have never been on a date quite like this one."

"Just a routine evening with old Scott. I will call you tomorrow after I see the sheriff in the morning."

We parted and I drove home on a cloud. I wasn't too worried about witnessing the bootlegging. Such activity had become commonplace and the Prohibition Amendment would likely be repealed when a few more states voted on the ratification of the repeal of it.

After calling ahead, I went to the sheriff's office as I told Sally I would. Horace Bogar had been sheriff of San Lucia County for as long as I could remember. He was popular with the pioneer cattlemen and citrus growers who had the money and wielded the power. My father fell into neither category.

His contacts with Sheriff Bo were largely confined to infrequent visits on Monday mornings to arrange the release from jail of one of his employees who may have overindulged on the previous Saturday night.

The sheriff's department was next to the courthouse, in a separate building with the county jail in back. To get there from where I parked, I walked alongside the jail where inmates were talking through the bars to family members and friends outside. The conversations were loud, sprinkled with laughter and some profanity. Reaching the front of the building, I entered the outer room where one of Sheriff Bo's henchmen, Jack Archer, was behind a desk reading a newspaper, drinking coffee and eating a doughnut, and a deputy, Hank Slade, was sitting in a straightback chair leaning against the wall. Hank's greeting was cordial. He was a special friend of my brother Bill. They played all sports together on the high school teams. Jake was absorbed in the newspaper.

"Go on in. The sheriff is expecting you," Hank said.

As I walked into his inner office, the sheriff greeted me, "Good mornin', Scotty, how you doin'? It's good to see you, boy. I understand you're gonna be up with the Gators this year. How you think they'll do?" Bogar gave me a politician's smile and handshake. I could tell that I was being patronized. He still thought of me as just another kid around town.

"The Gators should do very well, but I don't know how much longer Coach Bachman will be there. It's rumored that he might move to Army after the coming season."

"I'm sorry to hear that. Scotty, what can I do for you? My deputy says you got some information for me."

I related our experience of the night before near Manatee Creek, telling him that the girl with me was Lil Graham's cousin Sally, visiting from Atlanta. I added, "It looked to me like whiskey was being smuggled in from the Bahamas. While it's no secret that Sally Graham was with me, I would rather

her name be kept out of this."

"Well, it sounds like there was some bootleggin' goin' on. I hope you didn't recognize any of the guys on that beach. It mightn't be healthy for you and that little Georgia gal to know who they were. The bootleggers wouldn't like it if they thought that you could finger them with the feds."

For some reason, I withheld telling the sheriff that the boat looked familiar to me. I spent much of my spare time at Brackett's Boat Yard on Monroe Creek. Tom Brackett, in addition to playing trombone, builds a sturdy cabin cruiser with distinctive lines. I had remembered a new one launched this summer. The outline of the boat we saw that night resembled that of a Brackett Cabin Cruiser.

Obviously wanting the conversation to end, Sheriff Bo stood up at his desk, and said, "Well, thanks for comin' in, son. Sally's name won't be in the report. Those bootleggers are long gone by now, but I'll send one of my men down there to check it out. You come back again any time, and you keep those Gators goin'. See you."

As I was leaving the office, Jake Archer went in the door of the inner office. He seemed nervous about something. As for my visit with the sheriff, I felt that I had wasted my time. Passing the jail going to my car, I knew that lunch was being served by the sound of spoons hitting tin plates. The menu probably included grits left over from the morning breakfast. The informal family and friends visiting time was over.

Sally had wanted to go with me when I talked to the sheriff, but I convinced her that we should limit knowledge of her involvement in the experience. Of course, I'm sure that she and Lil had whispered about it until the small hours of the morning after I took her home.

Upon returning to the hardware store, I placed a call to Sally as I had promised. I picked up the telephone and gave the central operator the Grahams' number. Lil answered, and called Sally who had been waiting to hear from me. After briefly exchanging greetings appropriate to the mood we were in when we parted last night, I told her of my visit with the sheriff.

"Well, what did he say?" Sally asked.

"Sheriff Bogar was unimpressed. I suspect that he feels that bootlegging isn't much of a crime. He'll send a deputy down to investigate, but he doesn't expect to find anything. He advises that we keep quiet about this as we might be in some danger if the bootleggers found out that we were there."

"How could we be in any danger if the sheriff himself looks on this as being unimportant?"

"That's a good point, and obviously, I hope he was exaggerating. It was easy to convince him that we have no idea who those people were." We ended our conversation, and I went to work on chores Dad had waiting for me in the store.

Sally and I were together almost every evening going to movies, a barbecue at a back-country ranch, picnicking on the beach, sailing, and dancing at one of the area's nightspots. On Thursday afternoon, we played tennis on the city courts. Having been on the high school team, I played fair tennis. Against Sally, no matter how hard I played, I managed to win only a few games. She was good, and showed no mercy.

Even though Sally seemed to enjoyed being with me on what was becoming almost nightly dates, I sensed a reservation on her part that puzzled me.

CHAPTER 5

A week after the visit to the sheriff's office, I heard that a man's body had been found, washed up on the beach north of Fort Capron. This wasn't so unusual as it happened a couple of times a year. Along the coast, someone would fall off of a boat and drown. After the submerged body had been in the water for a while, it floated to the surface and washed up on to the shore. It was an ugly sight, because crabs, sharks, and other fish did to the dead body what came naturally to them.

According to an account in the Tribune, the local newspaper, the body was found with an anchor line wrapped tightly around it. The report further stated that the anchor was missing from the chain at the end of the line. After examining the remains, the county coroner had concluded that the death was a suicide, or possibly a murder. He had found a major contusion on the deceased's head, but could not determine whether the blow occurred before or after the unidentified person entered the water.

Responsibility for further investigation lay with the state attorney, Paul Cochrane, who had upset the incumbent, Joe Noland, in an election the year before. Joe, who had held the job for twenty years, was a close friend of the sheriff. Bogar's support of Joe in the election had not engendered any great fondness between the sheriff and the State Attorney Cochrane.

The evening of the day that the coroner's finding was reported, I went to the Grahams' home for Sally. Her Aunt Mamie met me at the door.

"Good evening, Mrs. Graham."

"Hello, Scotty. Sally is upstairs with Lillian. I'll tell her you are here. You two are seeing a lot of each other, aren't you?" Mrs. Graham observed.

"Yes, ma'am, I guess we are. I hope you don't mind. She's a pleasure to be with, and we seem to like a lot of the same things."

"We enjoy having her with us, but her mother called today and suggested that she should come home this week-end."

As I considered this bit of news, Mrs. Graham called up the stairs, "Sally, Scott is here." She and Lil must have heard me drive up, but she hadn't rushed down. Girls sometimes liked to have a date to wait a bit so as not to appear to be too anxious. I never minded as I usually got along well with the older folks while I was waiting.

Eventually, Sally came down the stairs wearing a pale green blouse, pleated white skirt and saddle-oxfords. "Hi, Scott. I'm sorry if I've kept you waiting," she said, with eyes shining in her beautiful face, which was framed by a dark page-boy bob.

"Oh, that's all right," I said casually, belying the little thrill I always felt when I saw her looking like that. "I've been enjoying a visit with your Aunt Mamie. I told her that we would be at the Beach Casino. We've seen the movie and there's nothing special going on tonight." The young crowd usually gathered there in the evening.

"Have a good time," Mrs. Graham said, "It was good to talk with you, Scotty, but don't keep her out too late."

"I won't, I have to be up early tomorrow," I said as Sally and I left to get in my car parked in the front of the Graham's house.

With Sally sitting closely beside me, we crossed over the Indian River but did not stop at the casino. Instead, we drove on to park on the dune overlooking the ocean, not far from where we had first met. I turned off the motor and turned on the radio. I placed my arm over her shoulder; she looked up at me and I kissed her. I sensed no reservation as she responded warmly. The top was down on my roadster, and for a while we just sat silently enjoying the loveliness of the starlit night.

"Did you see the paper today?" I asked finally, knowing that it was a subject we must discuss.

"If you mean, 'did I read about the body that washed up on the beach?' - yes, I did. You don't think that had anything to do with the bootlegging we saw, do you?"

"Sally, I just don't know. The coroner estimates that the body had been in the water a week. Word of our experience at Manatee Creek is getting around. If there was a murder, we may be in some danger. You should go home. I'm sorry I got you involved in this."

"You have nothing to be sorry about. That night that was one of the loveliest yet most exciting nights of my life. We're in this together, and you're not going to run me home to Mama," Sally said.

"Speaking of Mama, your Aunt Mamie told me your mother suggested that you return home this weekend. What's wrong with doing what your mother wants?"

"It's no use. I'm not a child anymore. This may be a serious situation we are in. I could no more abandon you than you could forsake me. If there is a problem, you need me and no one can help you like I can. So let's forget about my returning home, not at this time."

"I'll see Sheriff Bo again and make it clear to him that we have no idea who was doing the bootlegging, but I won't tell him that I recognized the boat, a cabin cruiser recently built by Brackett."

"Why not tell the sheriff that you recognized the boat? He can check the ownership, and that could lead him to the bootleggers, who may be murderers."

"I wish it were that easy. I came away from my other

meeting sensing an uncertainty based on the sheriff's attitude. We need to know whether or not there is a connection between the bootlegging and the murder."

"Didn't the article in the paper read that an anchor line was wrapped around the body, but that there was no anchor at the end of the chain?" Sally said.

"Yes, it did."

"Then, if the anchor line was wrapped around the body, and the body dropped overboard after we left, the anchor must have come loose, and must still be on the bottom of the ocean. If we go search and find the anchor near Manatee Creek, we can be reasonably sure that there is a connection."

What Sally said made sense, but it frightened me.

"Sally, even though the Manatee Creek area is isolated, the bootleggers, who may be murderers, would hear of it if we were diving in the ocean there."

"Then we need a cover story," Sally said. "Surely, you can think of something."

Our starlight talk continued but on a more romantic note, and later Sally and I joined our friends at the Beach Casino, where we danced to music played on the new nickel phonograph record machines. Our favorite number was Kenny Sargent singing "Under a Blanket of Blue" with Glen Gray's Casa Loma Orchestra.

We ended the evening early as Dad had me scheduled next day for an eight o'clock delivery in Okeechobee, a city thirty-five miles inland from Fort Capron. I said I would give some thought to a way we could dive in the ocean off Manatee Creek without arousing suspicion.

Our goodnight kiss was more than a peck on the cheek.

Before the bursting of the Florida boom, Okeechobee's name was changed to Okeechobee City, and was advertised in the northern press as a future metropolis. The natives continue to call the town Okeechobee. Much of the plumbing in the hastily constructed modern county courthouse was deteriorating and in need of replacing. By seven o'clock in the morning, Harcord Ritchey and I had loaded our Dodge truck with pipe and other supplies and we were headed west on Okeechobee Road.

On the narrow back-country road through the flat pinelands, studded with shimmering island-like hammocks, wading birds looked for breakfast in the ponds along the way. Just west of Five Mile, where Andrew and Maggie Graham lived, a great blue heron ascended majestically, frightened by the noisy truck.

"Much as I like the Indian River, I enjoy a visit to the back-country," I said to Harcord.

"It sure is pretty and peaceful," he replied. "Say, wasn't that Mr. Andy Graham's packing house back at Five Mile?" he added.

"It sure was. He and Miss Maggie have a nice home behind it under those big oaks surrounded by one of the best citrus groves in the county. I like to visit them when I can. Their nephew, Charles, stays out here with them every now and then."

Near Blue Field, where a pioneer family shared the area with neighboring Seminole Indians, water spilled over a small dam into the roadside canal. Experience told me that hungry bass were waiting for insects and minnows at the bottom of the little waterfall. To be prepared for such an opportunity, I always carried a fishing rod and reel in the truck with me.

Bringing the truck to a stop, while Harcord dozed on the seat I got out on the canal bank and cast a top-water plug near some lilypads close to the splashing water. It had only hit the surface when, with an aquatic explosion, a lunker bass knocked the plug high in the air. That fish was gone to strike another day. After a few more casts, I caught three smaller bass—just the right size for my frying pan. I put the fish in a croaker sack and anchored the sack with a stick in the edge of the water, intending to cook the fish for our lunch on our return this way at noon.

Continuing on to Okeechobee, we arrived at the courthouse and proceeded to unload the truck. Will Rawlings, a local lawyer whom I had hoped to see, stopped as he passed by on his way to his office. He and my father had been friends for years.

"It's good to see you, Scott," Mr.Rawlings said. "How're your folks?"

"Fine," I replied as Harcord and I took a temporary rest from our unloading. "Dad thought that I might bump into you today. He asked me to invite you and Mrs. Rawlings to have supper with us when you come to the sounding of the circuit court docket next Tuesday. Mother hasn't had a visit with Mrs. Rawlings lately, and Dad wants to talk to you about the gold coins and other artifacts that are said to be in the shallow water off the ocean beach. He knows that your interest in antiquities has led you to study old Spanish shipwrecks."

"Mrs. Rawlings and I would be most pleased to have supper with you. Yes, I find the stories of 16th century treasure-laden ships foundering in tropical storms along our coast to be most fascinating," Mr. Rawlings said. "I'll see you next week." He went on his way to his office.

Harcord and I finished unloading the truck and helped the plumbing contractor distribute the pipe and other material throughout the courthouse. It was almost noon when the county manager signed for the delivery, and we headed back to Fort Capron. Stopping where I had caught the fish, we found that the croaker sack with our lunch in it was missing. A big alligator lay on the edge of the opposite bank. I swear the gator was smiling.

"Well, it looks like that old gator has got our lunch," I said. "It has been a long time since breakfast. I suggest we stop at Five Mile and maybe we will get an invitation from

Miss Maggie to have a bite to eat."

Sure enough, when we stopped to visit Mrs. Graham shared with us some corn bread, ham, and collard greens that she had waiting for Uncle Andrew. I took the plates out on the steps of her front porch where Harcord was waiting, so as to avoid embarrassment for him or Miss Maggie.

Mr. Graham came over from the packing house. "Hello boys, "You look like you're enjoying that corn bread. Maggie makes the best there is," he said.

"Yes suh, we is, Mr. Andrew," Harcord said.

It was interesting to hear how Harcord lapsed into the Negro way of talking when he was around older white folks.

"Well, I'm glad. And how is your mother?" Mr. Graham replied.

"She's jus' fine. I'll tell her you asked about her."

We said our thanks to Mr. and Mrs. Graham, climbed in the truck, and headed for town.

While driving on to Fort Capron, I was thinking about my conversation with Mr. Rawlings, and it occurred to me that maybe we had the cover story we needed to look for the anchor. Why not spread the word that we were searching for treasure from one of the ancient shipwrecks?

"Have you ever seen anything on the beach that might have come from one of the wrecked treasure ships that are supposed to be off-shore around here?" I asked Harcord as we rode along.

"Well, as you know, I don't get to the beach much, and I can't say as I ever have, but I've always heard that some folks have."

"The idea of that treasure being out there intrigues me, and Mr. Rawlings says a wreck might be close to shore where the water isn't too deep. Some day I might pick a spot in the ocean where it's shallow, and with the right equipment, make a search of the bottom. It may sound foolish, but it wouldn't do any harm to try," I said, taking the first step in my campaign to spread the word.

We returned to the yard where Dad had plenty for us to do. He was using Harcord to the point where he was almost a full-time employee. Even though I was anxious to discuss my idea with Sally, I was too busy to call her, and would have to wait until I saw her that night. Besides, I knew that Sally and Lil would be sunning and swimming at the beach. Sally's mother had agreed to let her stay another week.

Finally, the work day ended, and I went home where Mother was in the process of fixing supper. After showering then dressing in my room upstairs, I joined Mother in the kitchen helping her finish the supper preparations.

"Did you have a good trip to Okeechobee today?" Mother asked, putting a lid on the pan of chicken she had been frying.

"Yes, and I saw Mr. Rawlings as you hoped I would. He accepted the invitation, and he and Mrs. Rawlings will be here Tuesday night," I replied. "Would it be all right if I asked Sally to join us?" I added.

"Of course," Mother said. "She's a nice girl and I'd like to get to know her better. Call your father and tell him that supper is ready." While waiting for Dad, Mother smiled as I rambled on about Sally.

Sally and I went to the movies that night. Before taking her to the Grahams', we stopped by Decker's for a snack. A carhop took our orders. Seated in the car, I asked Sally if she was familiar with the accounts of early Spanish shipwrecks along Florida's coastline.

"A little," she replied. "They were part of the history of the early explorations in our hemisphere, a subject we studied in school."

I proceeded to explain my plan to use an alleged search

for treasure to cover up the fact that we were actually diving to look for the anchor.

"Mr. Rawlings, a lawyer from Okeechobee, and his wife are having supper with my folks Tuesday night. He'll be talking with my father about his research into the wrecks of Spanish treasure ships along this coast. Mother was pleased to have me invite you to join us."

"I will be happy to come. It sounds like an interesting evening," Sally said.

"If during the evening I should just happen to suggest it, Mr. Rawlings will certainly encourage a search for such a wreck in the Manatee Creek area, and Dad will also. If we should make such a search, the word will circulate in no time that we are going to be diving in the ocean looking for treasure when we will really be looking for the anchor."

"Well, you've thought of a good cover-story, but wouldn't the reality of diving there be too much for us? How deep is the water?" she asked.

"If we dive at low tide, the water where that anchor is, if there is an anchor, with the sun out we can see clearly, especially if we use goggles like the motorcycle riders wear. Some of us have reached the bottom in water as deep as twenty-five feet, just taking dares."

"Then, let's do it," Sally said as the carhop brought our orders. Eddie and Nell came out from inside Decker's and seeing us, came up to the car and Eddie said, "We're going over to the Beach Casino. Why don't you all join us?"

"I'm bushed," I said. "It's been a long day".

"We'll see you later, alligator," Nell said as they got in her sister's car and drove off.

We finished the Alfred's chocolate ice cream we had ordered and drove to the Grahams' house. I took her to the door where I kissed her good night, and drove home hoping that our cover-story plan would work.

CHAPTER 6

When Mr. and Mrs. Rawlings came to dinner, during dessert and coffee Sally and I listened with genuine interest to the treasure ship discussions, even though we had an ulterior motive.

"Dad, has anyone around here made a serious effort to look for the wreckage of one of those ships?" I asked during a break in the conversation.

"Not that I know of," my father replied. "Folks just assume that this happened so long ago, the wrecks and treasure would be lost in deep water out in the ocean. Searching wouldn't be worth the effort."

"That wouldn't necessarily be so," Mr. Rawlings interjected. "If a ship had remained in the deep water, it wouldn't have foundered. Wreckage and treasure may be covered by sand, but some may be closer to shore than we think."

Trying not to appear too eager, I said, "I know it's a long shot, but I'd be willing to try a dive somewhere, and see what I could find."

When we finished our desserts, Mother cleared the table with Sally's help. Mother and Mrs. Rawlings retired to the drawing room, but at a sign from me, Sally joined me going into the den. Savoring the meal they had enjoyed, Mr. Rawlings and Dad sat in the soft leather chairs with which Mother had furnished the den, lit up cigars, and continued the discussion. Sally and I were on a settee across the room.

"Scott, you're talking about miles and miles of coastline; you wouldn't know where to begin," Mr. Rawlings said with a flick of cigar ash into a heavy tray Mother had provided.

I rose to the challenge and said, "Although the kids around here have been swimming a lot in the Manatee Creek area, we've not dived it because there's no coral reef. What if I began a search in that area? In the daylight, of course, not when bootleggers might be arriving, as we experienced the other night."

"Well, that would be as good a place as any to start," Mr. Rawlings mused. "If you do decide to do it, you should look for coins, jewelry, jars, copper pots, cutlery, or other such small articles on the ocean floor, even more so than evidence of the wreck."

"Why is that?" I asked.

"The boats were made of wood, and iron straps and nails. The wood would have rotted away and the iron rusted, but the gold, jewels, and glass and copper could be there yet. Some artifacts, buried in the sand long ago, may be uncovered from time to time by storms and changing currents."

"Even though we may find nothing, the idea of the search interests me. Dad, would you let me have a few days off so that I can give it a try? I'd need someone to help me. All of the guys are working, but Sally is available. She's a very strong swimmer, and it will give her a chance to do something very special on her vacation, something that apparently hasn't been done before around here. That is, if you are interested?" I asked Sally, knowing what her answer would be.

Dad agreed that I could take a few days off from work so that Sally and I could attempt to find treasure from a wrecked Spanish galleon. Suggestions were made as to what kind of equipment would be helpful in making the search. We settled on the use of goggles for better vision under the water and sash window weights to counter the water's buoyancy.

Mother and Mrs. Rawlings joined us and Mrs. Rawlings said, "Will, we must be running along. It's getting late and you have a long day tomorrow. Let's thank these dear friends for a good dinner and a pleasant evening. It was especially nice to be with the youngsters."

"Yes. I don't know when I've had such a good audience to listen to me ramble on about Spanish shipwrecks. I will be anxious to hear the results of their adventure," Mr. Rawlings said as they bade us goodnight and went to the hotel.

The next day, I telephoned the state attorney, Paul Cochrane, and told him what we were going to do and why. During the conversation, I was somewhat surprised to learn that the sheriff had said nothing to him of my report of the bootlegging at Manatee Creek.

"Maybe he was going to get around to telling me, but I have talked to Bo a couple of times and he didn't mention the incident," Cochrane said.

"Well, we saw no violence, and the sheriff certainly didn't appear concerned about the bootlegging."

"Few people are these days. However, you shouldn't be diving for the anchor. I'll arrange for a search to be made."

"No, I have a feeling that somebody in this town had something to do with bringing the whiskey in," I said. "I think it would be better if we went ahead with our plan to look for the anchor, making it appear that we are just searching for treasure."

"You may be right, but keep me posted. If you find the anchor, or see anything suspicious, get in touch with me anytime, day or night. This could be dangerous," the state attorney warned and hung up.

I talked to my father in his office about the time I would take off. Since I would be working only two more weeks, he needed to start breaking in someone to take my place anyway. He said I could start the search on Thursday. That was agreeable with Sally when I called her.

To avoid being subject to the vagaries of the wind, our transportation for the trips to and from Manatee Creek was the family's 16-foot launch, powered by a one-cylinder Palmer engine. She was a stable little craft with the classical Greek water nymph name of Undine painted on her transom. Included in the gear we put aboard was a small raft on which we could hang for rest between dives, and a square of canvas with poles to provide shade on the beach. We decided to take the sash weights even though we weren't sure how we would use them.

Stowing everything aboard, including sandwiches and drinking water, we left our dock at noon. Chugging along at a steady six knots, we arrived at Manatee Creek two hours before the ocean's low tide. The gear and supplies were carried through the trees and deposited on the beach. I busied myself arranging the gear when Sally stepped behind some sea grape bushes and changed into a bathing suit.

Determining the search area wasn't as simple as we had expected. We knew it would be south of where we were the night of the bootlegging, but the distance was difficult to judge. Even though the earlier scene had been illuminated by a brightly shining moon, we saw no landmarks that would be helpful. We tried to remember the volume of the sound of the voices we heard. Estimating that the smugglers' boat had landed at least two hundred yards down the beach, we chose a location north of that to set up our awning.

Having anchored the raft off-shore in chest-deep water, Sally stayed with it while I swam underwater with a sash-weight tied to fifteen feet of line lightly fastened around my waist. I wanted to be able to surface without hindrance. With the line held between my teeth three feet away from the weight, I easily swam near the ocean bottom, which was clearly visible with the goggles in place. I went out as far as I dared and then back beneath the raft, coming up for air when necessary.

We moved the raft twenty-five feet to the south after this

first survey and continued moving it the same distance south after subsequent trips. Sally made quick searches in the shallower water between the raft and the shore. After three round-trips, I searched the shallower water, and Sally took a turn going out. Although she had a problem using the sash-weight technique, she covered much of the bottom.

After two hours, we retired to the beach for a sandwich break. I went to the boat and finding some big snaps in a fishing-tackle box, I improved the sash-weight arrangement so that we did not have to hold the line between our teeth.

That we had found nothing was not discouraging. Our starting point had purposely been a conservative selection, so the most likely area was yet to be searched. Since we first entered the water, the falling tide had slacked and begun to rise. I suggested that Sally make the next underwater trip out from the raft before the water got any deeper.

We moved the raft another twenty-five feet to the south, and Sally put on the goggles, snapped on the line, and kicked her way to the sandy bottom. She surfaced for air and descended again. I turned to face the shore, preparing to search in the shallow water when I heard Sally scream, "Help! Help! Help!" Spinning around, I was stunned to see the dorsal fin of a shark cutting the surface of the water inshore from Sally and circling back toward her. Eyes wide with terror, Sally continued to scream.

"Stay still! Be still!" I yelled, swimming rapidly toward her. Approaching Sally, the shark was getting ever nearer, closing in for the attack. She shrieked as the shark reached her and veered on by. Sally was hysterical when I gathered her in my arms.

"You're all right now. The shark has gone, and won't come back if we calm down," I managed to say while unsnapping the sash-weight and doing my best to keep us afloat with Sally holding me so tight I could hardly breathe.

"But, I felt it! It hit me in the leg! I'm so scared," she said frantically, appearing to be about to lose control again.

"Roll over on your back, and try to relax. I'll swim you to the beach." She did as I said, and using a cross-chest carry I got her to shore where she lay shaking on a blanket trying to recover from the fright. An examination of her right leg revealed a light abrasion. Apparently the shark with its sand-paper-like skin had brushed against her as it passed. It was no wonder that she was hysterical.

Trying to soothe Sally by explaining that the shark was probably a sand shark, and would attack her only if it became excited by the smell of blood or the sight of thrashing legs. I added, "You were probably in no real danger."

"Well, how in the world was I supposed to know that?" she asked in a shaky voice. "The shark was headed my way and I was sure he was attacking. Feeling it scrape my leg, I thought it had actually bitten me. Never in my life have I been so terrified."

"I'm sorry," I said. "I should have warned you that this might happen. The sharks seldom appear unless bait-fish are in the water; since I had seen none, it didn't occur to me that a shark might be around."

Sally's diving was over for the day. She retired to the other side of the dune and changed from her bathing suit to a tee-shirt and shorts. She sat on the beach while I resumed the search. I saw no more of the shark, and after moving the raft twice more to the south, decided to end the search for that day. I had the feeling that tomorrow would have us in the area where we were most likely to find the anchor, if it were ever to be found by us.

We carried our gear to Manatee Creek and boarded the Undine. I choked and cranked the engine, starting it with the first pull. We motored homeward, admiring the panorama emblazoned in the western sky by the setting sun. Sally had forgiven me. It was a nice way to end an exciting day.

By the time I returned from taking Sally to the Grahams' house, I had missed supper with the family. A pot of chicken and dumplings was left simmering on the stove. After finishing the last of my favorite dish, I telephoned Paul Cochrane to tell him we hadn't found the anchor, but that the most likely area was yet to be searched.

"What makes you think that somebody in this town was involved in the bootlegging?" Paul asked.

"Because of the bootleggers' boat. In the bright moonlight, I could see by the outline of the hull and cabin that it was a Brackett Cabin Cruiser. I remember one that was recently launched, painted with a waterline somewhat higher than normal so that a heavy load of cargo aboard wouldn't be so noticeable. Tom told me that the higher water line was requested by the owner. I don't know who he was building it for, but that should be easy to determine."

"I'll check it out with Tom without mentioning your name. If you and Sally find an anchor, carefully mark its location, and come on home. You tell me where it is, and I'll go down and get it. For use in court, the anchor must be properly identified and the evidence preserved," Paul said.

Finishing the conversation, I assured Paul that I would do as he said. Sally had seen enough of me today, and I was tired. I talked with her briefly by telephone. Fearing that Mrs. Graham would stop her from continuing the search, Sally had told nobody of her encounter with the shark.

At three o'clock Friday afternoon, I had lengthened the sash-weight line and while swimming with the sun shining nearly overhead, I saw an anchor below me. It was about one hundred fifty yards out from shore, and twenty-five feet down in the deepest water I had yet searched. Surfacing and treading water, I shouted to Sally, "Yo, Sally. I see an anchor! Bring out the corks and line."

"Hooray!" Sally yelled. "Hang on! I'm coming." Sally had been resting on the beach. She swam out with a length of tarred line tied to fish-net corks. Considering the shark experience of the day before, she showed a lot of courage by coming out so far.

Diving once more with the help of the sash-weight, I went to the bottom and saw that no chain was attached to the anchor, and the shackle was missing. Taking time to carefully tie the marker line to the anchor, I experienced pressure in my ears and a tightness in my chest. Surfacing, I gasped for air. When my breathing normalized, I fastened the line from the anchor to the corks, but left enough slack so that the corks would show on the surface when the tide rose. We swam to the shore, excitedly exchanging congratulations for our success.

On the beach, I said, "I hate to bust our bubble, but the facts are that there was no chain attached to that anchor."

"Well, that's a sobering thought."

"Yes, considering all the other circumstantial evidence, murder is the only reasonable conclusion, and we probably saw the person or persons who did it. The fun and games are over. I do wish you were home in Georgia and not involved."

"We have been over all of this before," Sally said. "Knowing of the bootlegging, the body, and the missing anchor, we, in good conscience, had to follow through. No one else could have helped you with the cover story better than I. Let's return to town, tell Paul Cochrane what we have done, and he can take it from there."

She was right, of course. Taking a last look at the marker-corks out on the ocean's surface, we made our preparations to depart. After shooing me away, Sally went behind some sea-grape bushes, removed her bathing suit, and put on a blouse and shorts. My nobleness was getting to be too much. While she was changing, I took our belongings to the launch at Manatee Creek.

We boarded the Undine and stowed our gear. I pulled the choke, grabbed the knob of the Palmer's flywheel, and gave the engine a crank. It chugged twice, then stalled. Adjusting the choke, I pulled the crank again; still the engine didn't start. Turning the flywheel several more times produced nothing other than bruised knuckles. I expressed my displeasure with a few appropriate swear words, necessitating an apology to Sally.

"This motor has chosen a poor time to act up. The carburetor's probably clogged. I'll take it off and blow it out, and we should be going before long. Give me a sailboat any day."

Just as I was speaking of sailboats, a catboat was passing the mouth of the creek. It was Artie Thacker who works part time for Brackett, but makes extra money trolling for speckled trout on the river. He lives in a shack on the Brackett Boat Company property. Artie spotted us with our engine problem, and offered to take us home in his boat. Knowing how small the sailboat was and how it smelled, I declined, saying, "Thanks, but the carburetor just needs cleaning. I'll have us underway shortly." He sailed on, heading toward Fort Capron.

I reached for the toolbox which is usually stowed in the cuddy-cabin in the bow of the launch. It wasn't there. By then, Artie was beyond hailing distance. The absence of the toolbox perplexed me; it should have been aboard. There was no way I could clean out the carburetor without a wrench. I looked everywhere in the boat for a wrench or some pliers. I found pliers in the fishing-tackle box, but the jaws weren't big enough to fit the nut on the carburetor.

"I'm sorry to say that there's no way I can fix the engine," I told Sally. "For some reason the toolbox isn't in the boat. I can't clean the carburetor without a wrench." I cringed at the thought of what her response might be.

"That's all right. I'm sure you will get us home somehow," she said loyally.

"I can get us home, but it will take a while. I'm going to have to row."

The launch was equipped with oars and oar-locks. My father had insisted on this as a safety feature because he never completely trusted any engine, even the usually faithful Palmer engine. After making one more unsuccessful attempt at starting the engine, I shipped the oars and rowed out of the creek.

"We have more than five miles to go. I'll be rowing against the flood tide for about two hours, until it becomes slack. But then, with the tide ebbing, the current should be with us. The time is 4:30 now so we should be at our dock by 8:30," I explained to Sally.

"Can't I help?" Sally asked.

"Yes. I'll disconnect the steering wheel and you can guide us with the tiller so I can concentrate on rowing without worrying about the course. At the beginning, let's work our way out toward the center of the river. Maybe a boat will come along and give us a tow to home."

CHAPTER 7

Aided by a light southeasterly breeze, we began our long, slow journey home. With my feet braced against one of the launch's ribs, I put my back to the task of pulling on the long oars. Fortunately, my hands were toughened by the work I had been doing in the lumberyard. Sally was in the stern ably performing her assignment of holding the boat on its proper course. As she commented cheerfully about the jumping mullet and the pelicans plunging into the water, I was able to enjoy her gentle smile and the reddish highlights in her hair reflecting the afternoon sun. To my surprise, a boat appeared behind us, coming from around Summerlin Point south of Manatee Creek. I had hoped for a tow, but hadn't expected the possibility of one quite so soon.

"Sally! Look behind you. There's a boat and it's headed this way. Let's wave something at them."

As the craft drew closer, I could see that it was a sizeable sea-skiff with a small cabin forward piloted by Sheriff Bogar's deputy, Hank Slade. Coming out of the boat's cabin was Jake Archer.

"Hello there! Aren't you Scotty Forrester? Looks like you got a problem. It's a mighty long row to Fort Capron," Archer said, walking to the stern of the boat.

"Yes, sir. Our engine is clogged up and I don't have the tools to fix it. If you've got a wrench I could use, I should be able to get it going," I replied.

"No need to do that. Just hop aboard here, and we can hide your boat over in the mangroves. It'll be safe tonight, and you can come back for it tomorrow. We'll run you home before your folks start worrying about you. It's getting late.

I didn't like that suggestion but there wasn't much I could do but take him up on his offer. It could have been that the deputy was just investigating the bootlegging, yet in the back of my mind, I had the feeling that they had been spying on us. It made me wonder if they had anything to do with the engine trouble and the absence of the toolbox.

I introduced Sally to Jake Archer, and the deputy, Hank Slade. My friends thought of Hank as a nice guy. When he played on the San Lucia County High School football team, Hank was good enough to get a scholarship at Oglethorpe University in Georgia.

Leaving the diving gear and the raft in the launch, we handed our things to Hank and clambered aboard the cruiser. Hank towed Undine to the mangroves, where we hid it as Jake had suggested. With Jake on a copilot's chair alongside him, Hank advanced the throttle, getting underway.

"I heard you all were doing some divin' for treasure," Jake said, turning to Sally and me on the back seat where we were sitting, "Did you have any luck?"

"No, not yet. But we're planning to keep trying this weekend. Will Rawlings thinks that there must have been some wrecks along here somewhere. Sally is going home to Georgia next week, and she's spending her last vacation days as a treasure hunter. Although the odds aren't so good, maybe we'll get lucky, and she can take a gold necklace back with her as a souvenir."

I was impressed with the quietness of the sea-skiff's motor. In answer to my query, Hank said the boat was powered by a Buick engine, muffled for surveillance. That explained why we hadn't heard them while we were diving.

We soon reached the channel in the middle of the river, but instead of turning north, Hank steered south. I didn't like this at all.

"Where are we heading?" I asked.

"Hank's going to drop me off at the community dock in Walton," Jake said. "I've got an appointment in Jensen. Hank will take care of you." Walton was a fishing village on the mainland between Fort Capron and Jensen.

Jake disembarked on the Walton wharf. Had there been anyone on the dock, Sally and I would have tried to hitch a ride to Fort Capron. I had begun to feel more like needing a rescue than being rescued. No one was there so we stayed aboard. A car was at the foot of the wharf. Jake got in it and drove off.

Hank piloted the boat away from the dock toward the river channel. Instead of heading north toward home, he turned south. As I started to protest, Hank pulled a pistol out, and ordered us into the cabin.

"Hank, what are you doing? Put that gun away!"

"I hate doin' this to you, but Bo told us we should be lookin' for you, and to bring you in if we found you. Darned if I know what's goin' on. Before Jake got off at Walton, he told me to take you somewheres else, but not to let you know where. Get in that cabin. I'll crack the forward hatch so's you'll get some air," Hank said.

The frightening sight of the gun being pointed at us convinced me, so we went below and sat on a bunk where Sally held my hand tightly. She was scared, but not crying. Having no portholes, the cabin was completely dark and I found no switch on the cabin light above us.

"Sally, what can I say except that I am so very sorry. I let my ego take over my brain, trying to be the hero who brought the bad guys to justice and now look at the mess I've gotten you into. How could I have been so stupid?"

"Don't blame yourself. I could have backed out of this at any point. Apparently, our cover story didn't fool the sheriff, and he is mixed up in this in some way. Let's quit dwelling on how stupid we are, and concentrate instead on being smart enough to get out of this mess."

"I love you, Sally. I promise that nothing bad is going to happen to you, even if my life depends on it," I said, putting my arm around her.

I could not see her in the darkness but I felt her looking at me as she replied, "That means more to me than you can possibly know, but there is something I must tell you. I haven't told you before because I wasn't absolutely sure where this was going; it is only fair that I tell you now. I am engaged to a young man in Atlanta that I have known a long time. Our families, and everyone, including me, has assumed that we will marry now that I am out of high school."

I was absolutely stunned. "You can't mean that," I said.

"I don't know what I mean. Since meeting you I have been very confused. John—that's his name—never made me feel the way you do. When you and I part in the evening, I can't wait to see you again. Maybe my emotions are caught up in the adventure and this will pass, but I don't think so."

I did the only thing I could think of to do. There, in that dark cabin, I kissed her. Our lips parted. Sally said with a sigh, "What am I going to do?"

Returning reluctantly to the immediate problem, I said, "We'll get back to that later, but what we must do now is use our wits. It's very important to know where Hank takes us. Dark as it is, I can't read my watch, but if we concentrate we can estimate the passage of time. It was seven o'clock when we left the dock at Walton. About now, the folks back home will start worrying. I told them that we would be back early since I am to attend a meeting at the church tonight."

"Yes, and Aunt Mamie expects me for supper."

After cruising along at about fifteen knots for what we estimated to be a half an hour, Hank slowed the boat and banked to the right. Upon leveling off, he opened the throttle, resuming the original speed. According to my calculations, we had passed Jensen and rounded Sewall's Point into the San Lucia River. I was relieved somewhat, as I was afraid Hank might have been told to take us across the Gulf Stream to West End, a Bahamian settlement on the westerly tip of Grand Bahama Island. The distance was such that he could have easily reached the Bahamas before dawn on a calm night like this.

We were headed northwest behind Sewall's Point preparing to bear to the left as we proceeded inland on the San Lucia River. The river has two forks. The south fork is a part of a cross-state waterway system connecting the Atlantic Ocean with the Gulf of Mexico by way of Lake Okeechobee. The north fork begins as a wide estuary, narrowing to a jungle-like river meandering its way through moss-draped live oaks and cypress trees to its headwaters behind Fort Capron.

We turned right entering the north fork. As we cruised the estuary, I could hear distant thunder rumbling in the west. After about twenty minutes, Hank backed the throttle down to slow speed, then to idling before killing the engine. Without seeing out, I was reasonably sure that we had motored up to a dock at the old Fultz place at Spruce Bluff.

The west side of the northerly end of the estuary we had just navigated was bordered by a high sand bluff topped with dwarfed white pine trees called Florida spruce and cabbage palm trees, and patches of scrub palmetto. In 1889, one John E. Fultz brought his family from South Carolina, and homesteaded 180 acres at that location. Other families followed, making their homes there. The settlement was abandoned in 1906 after efforts to cultivate the sandy soil were unsuccessful.

With a dock nearly hidden in the mangroves, the Fultz house still remained on the top of the bluff among the spruce, and a strand of stately royal palms which were old when Fultz arrived. Being accessible only by boat, few people knew the place was there. When hunting quail with my father a few years before, we had stopped at Spruce Bluff.

Holding the gun on us Hank made Sally and me blindfold each other with kerchiefs before letting us out of the boat's cabin.

"Jake said that I wasn't supposed to let you know where you were," he said while checking our blindfolds.

Hank led us from the boat along the narrow dock through the mangroves to the shore. I could hear the alligators nearby as they slithered through an adjacent marsh and splashed into the water. We stumbled along a path to the house.

It was about eleven o'clock when Hank steered us to the old house. He said, "Scott, this is where we part company. There's a couple of men here that's supposed to guard you. Like I said, I don't know what's goin' on, I'm just doin' what Jake told me to do. Jobs are hard to find these days, and I need this one." I heard more distant thunder.

A person with big hands led us inside the house and removed our blindfolds. By the light of a kerosene lamp, we could see that one of our guards was a small white man with close-cropped hair, no one that I could recognize. The other guard was the man with the big hands, whom I determined to be a Bahamian by the way he talked after removing our blindfolds. I had no doubt that in a fair fight, I could take the little guy, but I didn't know about the other one. With the friendly smile on his black face, he didn't look so tough, but he was big.

"All right, you kids, you're going to be staying right here with Rollie for a while. You'll be sorry if you try something stupid. I'm leaving now, but he'll be locking you in a room upstairs," the white man said. We heard him leave with Hank as the boat pulled quietly away.

"We are going to get along fine jus' so you don' cause no trouble," Rollie said. "Ah have been tol' dat ah was to keep you here, and not let you get away."

"We were brought here by gunpoint against our will," I said. "I'm sure our folks don't know where we are. They're going to be worried, and whoever is responsible for this will be the ones in trouble. You don't want to get into trouble, do you?"

"How kin ah get into any trouble? D'mon dat brought you here is a deppity sheriff. Ah 'mit ah wondered why you was blindfolded, but I figgered dat mus' be da way it was s'posed to be since Sheriff Bo had you brought down. I been working fo' him over in dah islands."

"What do you do for him in the islands?" I asked.

"Oh, dat's a secret; ah cahn't tell nobody. If you need to go to dah outhouse, ah kin let you go out, one at a time."

Rollie handed us a flashlight and I gave it to Sally so she could take advantage of Rollie's offer.

"Jus' go out the back door an' wit dah light, you can see dah path to dah facility."

"You come on in to dah kitchen an ah'll git you younguns something to eat," Rollie said, keeping an eye on me.

Sally returned from the outhouse and joined us in the kitchen, where Rollie had fixed each of us a ham sandwich made with Bahama bread. He had also poured us some milk from a pitcher in an old icebox. The way we wolfed down the sandwiches and milk made us realize how hungry we were. I went to the outhouse leaving Sally watched over by Rollie.

Having been there before, the area was generally familiar to me, but I could recall very little detail. The old royal palms were closer to the house than I remembered.

Even though I had heard occasional thunder in the distance, the sky above was clear and there was some light from a waning moon. With the help of the flashlight, I could make out the remains of other Spruce Bluff houses and sheds standing in various stages of disrepair. In the middle of the settlement was a cemetery, hauntingly beautiful among the dwarfed white pines. Tombstones, some erect and others tilted, marked the graves of children and adults who, around the turn of the century, had succumbed to the ravages of untreated diseases, accidents, and old age.

Sally and Rollie were in the kitchen when I returned to the house. "It's time you two was upstairs. Ah's gonna have to lock you in so's I can get some rest."

Sally thanked Rollie for the food as we went up the stairs with him following. At the end of a hall toward the rear of the house was a room with a stout door. Rollie handed us the flashlight and locked us in the room.

Inside, I shined the light around and saw that it was furnished with very old furniture including a chiffonnier, a Morris chair, a straight chair and a double bed, all probably left from the Fultz days.

For the first time since we were brought to the house, I could talk to Sally alone. "Don't be fooled by the Bahamian's friendly attitude. He probably doesn't know what has happened up to now, nor realize the seriousness of the situation. Deputy Hank Slade and Rollie claim that they don't know what this is about. Jake Archer, the sheriff's henchman, surely knows."

"Well, what do you think is going on? Why have they done this to us?" Sally asked.

"We witnessed events leading up to a murder, and our search for the anchor has spooked the person or persons responsible. It definitely looks like the sheriff was involved. Something had to be done about us, so here we are penned up in an old abandoned house."

"Our folks will be very worried since we did not return as expected," Sally said as she sat down on the edge of the bed.

"A search must be underway by now, probably organized by Paul Cochrane, who was aware of our plan. Paul warned us that something like this might happen." I surveyed the room looking for a way to escape.

"Looking for us must be awkward for the sheriff," I continued, "but he will have to go through the motions. Bo can't let it be known that his men are holding us. We could be here for days without anyone knowing it. We have to get out tonight."

I checked the windows and found that the only one not boarded up was a rear window about fifteen feet above the ground.

"We can't hope to escape through the rear window. The house is built on a ridge that slopes sharply at the back. A drop from this height would risk serious injury." I saw far-off lightning strikes in the western sky followed shortly afterwards by more thunder. "From the looks and sound of things, the back-country is experiencing quite a storm."

The letdown of captivity following a very strenuous eighteen hours made us realize how very tired we were. We needed at least a brief rest to be better able to plan our escape. Using the flashlight, I could see by my watch that the time was eleven-thirty.

"Sally, let's try to get some rest. You sleep on the bed and I will rest in the Morris chair."

Sally would have none of that. "I'm tired, and I'm scared," she said. "I want very much for you to hold me." We took off our shoes and stretched out on an old quilted comforter which was spread on the bed. Sally put her head on my shoulder and went to sleep in my arms.

Startled by an ear-splitting thunder-clap, we awoke in the fury of a storm that I thought would be confined to the back-country. I jumped from the bed and went to the window.

Continuous lightning flashes in the dark revealed the towering palms bent to the wind shreiking through the trees. Torrential rain drummed on the tin roof of the old house.

"Scott! What's happening?" Sally cried.

"Shh, it's all right," I replied, holding her in my arms while trying to calm her down even though I was scared myself. "A summer squall has moved in from the Everglades. It won't last long."

The wind began to blow even stronger. I could tell by the howl that it was reaching hurricane force. Then, I heard it coming! First there was just a cracking sound that grew louder until with a crash I felt a jarring force hit the roof with a tremendous jolt. One of the old royal palms had blown over on to the house.

Releasing Sally, I grabbed the flashlight and saw that the trunk of the tree was next to the window with the crown above the edge of the roof.

"Get your shoes on; this is our chance!" I shouted to Sally. She did as I said and went to the window.

"See," I pointed, "we can go out the window and crawl feet-first down the trunk of the tree to the ground."

"Oh, I don't think I can do that," Sally wailed as she saw the frightening scene below.

"Yes, you can. The storm has let up some since that big gust. I'll go out first and hold you as we slide down."

I climbed out the window and wrapped one leg around the trunk and, using the palm fronds, pulled myself to a precarious position on the tree. Just as she was taking my hand to join me, we could hear Rollie pounding on the door.

"I can't get dah door open. Is you all right?" he yelled.

We didn't try to answer, even if we could have. He continued to try to break the door down while we maneuvered down the tree to the ground. We had to find a place to hide because we knew he would come looking for us as soon as he got the door open and found that we were missing.

I thought of a place where we could hide. Taking Sally's hand and dragging her through the rain, we went to the cemetery and crouched behind some tombstones. "If I know Bahamians, Rollie won't come in here looking for us. They believe in ghosts."

The wind and rain eased up as the storm moved on as suddenly as it had come. In a little while Rollie came out of the back door of the house. He stood there looking one way and the other, and then, after a cursory glance toward the cemetery, headed south along the ridge. Sally and I left the cemetery using the flashlight we had taken from the room. That, and the small amount of moonlight, would provide the illumination needed to make our way north to safety.

In the sky was the constellation, Big Dipper, which aided me in locating Polaris, the North Star, which would be our guide as we hiked toward our destination—and a long hike it would be.

"Why did Rollie go south?" Sally asked while I stopped to take our bearings.

"He probably thought we would try to make it to Palm City because the walking is easier that way and nearer to civilization. Besides, there must be some way he could contact Sheriff Bogar, if necessary, and maybe it is in that direction," I replied.

Upon learning that we had escaped, Sheriff Bo would assume that our destination would be Citrustown, an agricultural settlement on the upper reaches of the north fork of the San Lucia River. The Citrustown general store stayed open all night to accommodate the local farmers. The sheriff would be certain that we would not attempt to get there on the river. No motor boats were available, isolated as we were, and rowing and paddling up the winding river in an abandoned boat we might find was not practical.

The sheriff would search for us on land with his new swamp-buggy, a vehicle with huge tires, built high off of the ground to allow passage through water-filled swamps and bogs. Apprehending us would be easy if we tried to get to Citrustown.

I decided that we could best elude the sheriff by heading for the home of Sally's Uncle Andrew at Five Mile on Okeechobee Road. The road to Okeechobee curved to the southwest from Fort Capron, so that Five Mile was not much further from Spruce Bluff than Citrustown. Undoubtedly my folks had reported us missing and others than the sheriff would be looking for us.

To go to Five Mile we were faced with the arduous task of traversing the back-country for twelve miles, walking through and around piney woods, sloughs, cypress swamps and scrub palmetto patches. This was the habitat of panthers, wildcats and bears; alligators lurked in swampy places. But the most dangerous of all the animals were the wild hogs preying on stray calves grazing the open range. Serious consequences could result if, in the darkness, a pack of hogs mistook us for strays.

At the outset, we made good time on the sand lands bordering the floodplain of the river. Our first challenge was to cross Cane Slough Creek. Upon hearing a bull gator bellow a love song to a lady gator in the marsh, we crossed the creek as far from the river as we could without going too much out of the way. Beyond the creek, we found the footing surprisingly good as we walked through the cabbage palms and gumbo-limbo trees. The night sounds were symphonic.

"Are there rattlesnakes out here?" Sally asked nervously as we walked along at a pretty good clip on the drier ground.

I answered in the affirmative.

"How are we to keep from stepping on one?"

"Since we were unable to see them, there is little we can do to avoid them except listen for the warning rattle. If we hear one, stand perfectly still. It is then that the snake is coiled and ready to strike at anything that moves," I told her.

"Don't worry, I won't breathe. I probably couldn't."

Even though I was pleased with our progress, I knew that with the terrain and distance ahead of us, we would be lucky to arrive before dawn. The land underfoot changed from sandy to soft damp soil, indicating that we were approaching another tributary creek. The weak glow of the waning moon revealed a grove of water oaks, their limbs draped with Spanish moss. Leading the way, I had just reached the creek when a blood-curdling scream split the air. My first thought was that something had happened to Sally. As I turned around, she threw herself into my arms, nearly knocking me down. The scream came again, sounding like the wail of a frightened young girl. Shining the flashlight behind us, I saw a form with two red orbs reflecting the light stretched out on a limb above. In the trees, ready to pounce, was a panther.

Dousing the light, I backed slowly toward the creek with my arm around Sally, holding her closely. Snarling as it came, the panther crept out on the limb in our direction. I had nothing I could use for a weapon. Sally pressed the side of her face into my chest, hypnotically watching the animal in the tree. Upon reaching the end of the limb, the panther attacked. As we dropped to the ground terrified, the cat glided overhead, landing on the back of an unfortunate yearling deer drinking from the creek. Grateful for our deliverance, we lay still with our hearts pounding, hearing the panther drag away its squealing prey.

The pitiful sound receded into the surrounding glade. Having covered her with my body, I lifted myself off of Sally. Weak from fright, I had difficulty standing. Every muscle in my body had tensed like a tight spring when I thought the panther was attacking us. With the passing of the danger, the spring released, leaving me limp.

I pulled Sally up into my arms. Eventually, we were able to go on. We crossed the little creek and collapsed in an open place beneath the oaks. Sally was shaking, more fatigued than she was willing to admit. It was time to stop.

Resting under the oak trees, we resisted the urge to close our eyes for much-needed sleep. Having finally calmed down, Sally did doze off for a few minutes. I gently shook her awake.

"Sally, we must keep moving. If we don't get to your uncle's house before daybreak, we might not get there at all."

"I know, Scott, but this is so peaceful. Let's stay here forever."

"If you are still asleep, that's a dream I would gladly share. Who knows? Maybe, when this nightmare is over we can plan a future of our own."

I pulled Sally to her feet and, bearing west of Polaris, we hiked on, rejuvenated by the brief rest. The rough terrain changed to pine land carpeted with grasses grazed on by open-range cattle making the walking easier, so we stepped up our pace. As the sky lightened in the east, on the horizon there appeared the canal bank which I had been expecting to see.

"There's the canal that extends south from your Uncle Andrew's place. It's Rim Ditch, a part of a local agricultural drainage district system, storing water in the dry months and protecting the interior lands from flooding during the rainy season. Your uncle's grove and packing house is located on Okeechobee Road only a short distance within the district. I don't know how far we are from Okeechobee Road, but a dirt road on the top of the bank will take us there."

"Do you mean that we've actually made it?"

"Well, not quite yet, but soon we will have."

Eventually we arrived at Rim Ditch and climbed the bank to the road. "Now, we need only to walk north. It should be no more than a couple of miles.

Let's go. The sun is rising. I've felt safe from the sheriff's men in the darkness, but being out here in the daylight makes me uneasy.

The sheriff has probably been looking for us along the San Lucia but by now he'll know that we came this way. We must get to your uncle's house and safety as fast as we can. I'll phone Paul Cochrane from there. As state attorney, he can call on the governor to get us protection, and begin an investigation of the entire affair."

As we proceeded north along the canal bank road, we saw in the distance a vehicle heading toward us. "Sally!" I said. "Get down the bank fast! A car is coming. It could be anybody. Until we know who's in that automobile, we'd better hide."

I was greatly relieved and certainly surprised to see Paul Cochrane alone in his Model-A Ford sedan. As he passed, I jumped up and called out his name. Paul hit the brakes and the car slid to a stop.

"Scotty! Sally! Thank goodness I've found you!" Paul said as he climbed out of the car. "Are you all right?"

"We're fine," I replied, "just a little tired is all. How did you happen to be way out here?"

"I'm looking for you guys. The whole town is worried. Organized searches were started at midnight, mostly over on the island, because Artie Thacker reported that he tried to bring you home when your boat broke down at Manatee Creek. But just a while ago, I overheard one of Bo's deputies telling how you had been picked up and taken to the old Fultz house down on the San Lucia, and that you had gotten away. Since you'd escaped somehow, I knew I had to find you before Bo did. He sent boats on the North Fork, and a swamp buggy on the land bordering the west side of the river, looking for you. I figured that you were too smart to try to get home that way. It seemed to me most likely that you would walk out here, go to one of the farms, and call in."

"Well, we're glad to see you. We've been mighty lucky thus far, but there've been times when I was afraid that our luck might run out."

We both started to get in the rear seat of the car, but Paul said, "Scotty, you get up front with me. Sally can stretch out and get some rest. She must be very tired." It seemed a little strange to me that he would want to separate us, but after helping Sally in the rear door, I walked around and got in the passenger seat beside Paul.

Paul started the engine, yet made no attempt to turn around. I asked him why we were heading south. He said, "If we try to turn around on the top of the bank, we might get stuck. Down a little further is a place we can make a U-turn."

I began to tell Paul of our kidnapping and escape from the old Fultz place. About fifteen minutes passed, yet we continued to drive away from Okeechobee Road.

"How much further do we have to go before we can head back?" I asked. I was anxious to get to Andrew Graham's place so we could call home.

"Not far now. Just take it easy, I'll have you and Sally safe in no time."

Before long, we came to a wide place in the road where a bridge extended across to the west side of the canal. Instead of turning around, Paul drove across the bridge and stopped the car.

I turned to ask what he was doing, and found myself staring into the barrel of a .30-caliber revolver. A gasp sounded from the rear seat. For the second time in a few hours, Sally was seeing a gun pointed at me.

CHAPTER 8

I was more depressed than frightened as I realized the reason for the apprehension that had been building within me since getting in the car. Once again, we were being abducted, not rescued.

"Scotty, don't you move! Sally, get out and open Scotty's door," Cochrane ordered.

"No! I won't," she said stubbornly. "I'm staying right here, and if you want the door opened, you do it."

Cochrane reached back to slap her, but stopped when he saw me looking for a chance to grab the gun. He then pointed it at Sally, slid out of the driver's seat, opened the left door and pulled Sally out of the car. Grabbing her by the arm, he led her around the front of the car and opened my door. I got out. Paul handed Sally a pair of open handcuffs.

"Put these on Scotty," he commanded.

"I will not!" Sally replied indignantly.

I held out my wrists to Sally. "You might as well put them on. With that gun, he's in charge." Sally took the handcuffs and put them around my wrists without closing them tightly.

"I see what you're trying to do. Snap them shut." Cochrane wouldn't get close enough to me to do it himself. He threatened her with the gun, and she closed the cuffs.

"Why are you arresting me?"

"I am not arresting you. You and Sally are going for a little ride, that's all." He continued to hold the gun on me as Sally got back into the rear seat.

Riding along a rutted road, I tried to think of a way to get us out of this mess. As we bounced along, I could have opened the door and rolled out and run, but that would have left Sally alone with Paul.

"Paul, what are you doing?"

"You saw too much that night on the beach, and would have eventually found out that the man who ordered that boat from Brackett is a friend of mine from Lacaya in the Bahamas. He had it built for me. Behind the scenes, I've been running the bootlegging and gambling in this part of Florida for three years. I needed the money for the campaign last year and to quietly build a political organization throughout the state."

"But what do you need a state-wide organization for? Your district just covers three counties."

"Do you think that I'm going to be the state attorney the rest of my life? No, sir! I'm going to be Governor Paul Cochrane after the next election. Nothing is going to stop me. I mean nothing," Paul said ominously. "Everybody is looking for you everywhere, except out this way. I can't let them find you because you now know that someone was killed that night. It was a guy from Miami who was trying to blackmail me."

The road ended at an old mined-out lime pit, partially filled with water. Beyond the pit was a hammock dense with live oak trees. Paul stopped the car and ordered us out. Sally ran to me, her eyes frightened. As Paul got out and walked around the front of the car, I whispered to Sally, "He's going to kill us, if we let him. I don't know what it'll be, but I'll try something. When I do, you run as fast as you can."

"You know you can't get away with this," I said to Paul.

"Oh, yes I can. Nobody ever comes out here this time of year. Your bodies may not be found for months. Now march toward that hammock."

We did as he said. Sally was in front of me; Paul was behind. Between this little parade and the hammock was the lime pit. A desperate plan formed in my mind. As we walked around the edge of the pit, I folded my cuffed hands in front of me and stopped suddenly. Following closely, Paul bumped into me. I swung my arms around and knocked him into the pit.

"Run, Sally, run," I yelled. Paul still had the gun. From the pit, he fired off a round. I felt the wind as the bullet passed my ear. Sally was running. Before Paul could pull the trigger again, I was on top of him. We struggled in the slimy lime. He slipped away from my grasp and pointed the gun at me. With my manacled hands, I grabbed the wrist of his gun hand. My head roared as he landed blows to my head with his free fist. My hands were slipping; I lost the grip. The roaring became even louder. Instead of feeling a bullet's impact, I was engulfed in a thick fog. My eyes burned, and I could barely breathe. Is this how it feels to die? I thought.

"Scott! Scott!" I could hear Sally cry frantically, her call coming as from a distance. The thought of leaving her made me hold on.

Through the haze, I crawled a few feet to where I could hear Paul coughing and gagging. He was crouched on his hands and knees, groping for the gun. Once again I threw myself on him, pinning him to the slime. Being bigger than Paul, there was no way that I was going to let him get up, but with the handcuffs on, there was nothing else I could do.

A few moments later, I heard Sally yelling, "They're down there! They're down there!"

Someone jumped into the pit, yanked me off Paul, rolled him over with his face in the lime, and handcuffed his hands behind his back. To my amazement, I saw that it was Sheriff Bogar's deputy, Hank Slade.

I clambered out of the lime pit, and there was Sheriff Bo himself. Hank dragged Paul, slipping and sliding, out of the pit and handed him over to two men who were standing by, one of whom looked familiar. With relief showing on his weathered face, the sheriff walked over to me and removed my handcuffs.

My bewilderment was interrupted as Sally, who had waited impatiently for me to be freed from the handcuffs, nearly knocked me down when she ran into my arms. "Oh, Scott! When I heard the shot, I thought he'd killed you," she cried, almost in hysterics.

"It was close, but he missed. What happened here?" I asked, still holding her to me.

"I'm not sure," Sally replied. "You'll have to ask them."

Looking around, I saw a Stearman biplane, engine idling, parked in a nearby open field. Two cars, including the sheriff's big Lincoln Phaeton, were on the road. I finally realized that one of the two men walking Paul Cochrane over to the other car was the little guy at the Fultz house last night. Making the cast of unexpected characters complete was Jake Archer with Sheriff Bogart.

"Get yourself cleaned up, and you and Sally get in my car. We're going back to Andrew Graham's house, and phone your folks. They're mighty worried. I'll fill you in on the way," the sheriff said.

Jake threw me a towel and I wiped the wet lime off as well as I could. Sally and I got in the back of the Lincoln while Jake took the driver's seat with the sheriff beside him.

Hank Slade went over to the biplane and climbed into the front cockpit. Painted on the side of the plane was "Hersey Crop Dusting." The pilot in the rear cockpit revved up the engine, taxied to the other end of the open field in which he had landed and turned around. After bouncing along the rough terrain, the airplane took off.

Waiting until the crop-duster plane was safely away, Jake started the Lincoln, driving slowly along the ruts toward the bridge. The other car with Paul Cochrane in it had gone on ahead of us.

Sheriff Bo turned from the front seat, and said, "Scotty, you and your girl are mighty hard to protect. Because of what you told me about the bootlegging, I knew that you and Sally had witnessed a murder when that body washed up on the beach. I'm not as dumb or as bad as you think I am. That's mostly an act, so that I can do my job effectively.

"You sure had me fooled," I said. "I guess Sally and I owe you our lives."

"You don't owe me nothin'. As a matter of fact, the way this turned out, I owe you. If you hadn't come to me in the office that morning, I wouldn't have had anything to go on. With those federal agents in the other car, we've been working for months trying to break up this bootleggin' and gamblin' operation. Several arrests have been made, but they were only minor players in the organization. The kingpin, whoever he was, stayed a couple of jumps ahead of us.

"The events followin' the murder at Manatee Creek provided us with the break that we were lookin' for. Tom Brackett told us that you recognized the boat on the beach that night. Through him we were able to tie it to Cochrane."

"I remember telling Dad about the boat. He must have told Tom," I said.

"Brackett told us that he built that boat for a British subject livin' at Lacaya on the south side of Grand Bahama Island. We have some Bahamians workin' for us over there. You met Rollie, one of our best, last night."

"I want to put in a good word for him," interjected Sally. "He was kind to us and it wasn't his fault that we got away."

"Thanks. I'll tell him you said that. Anyway," Sheriff Bo continued, "we learned that Paul Cochrane visited in the home of the Briton on at least four different occasions. These visits coincided with large deliveries of whiskey in our area. With other evidence we had, this confirmed our suspicion that Cochrane was the head of the bootleggin' ring.

"We figured that you had told Cochrane about recognizin' the boat. The word around town was that you were going to be diving for treasure near Manatee Creek. It was clear to us that you were really lookin' for the missin' anchor.

"We were concerned for your safety because you would be the principal witnesses against Cochrane, whom we suspected was in on the murder. He would have to get rid of you. We wanted to protect you without tippin' him off. The best solution we could come up with was to grab you and hold you overnight until we could arrest Cochrane. That's why we had Jake and Hank watchin' on the island."

Crossing the bridge over Rim Ditch, Jake drove north along the top of the bank. Without taking his eyes off the road, Jake said, "We saw you find the anchor. Hank clogged the gas line in your engine and took your toolbox so you couldn't find it. Artie Thacker almost messed up our plan, but you let him go on home without you. I reported to Bo while Hank took you to the Fultz place. You created a major problem when you got away and nearly got yourself killed."

"I assume my father must have reported us missing. What did you do about that?" I asked.

"Your dad and Brackett went down the river lookin' for you after Artie told them he had seen you, and that you were havin' engine trouble. It was midnight before they called our office to report you missin'. After that call, the whole town knew it. Betty Foster, our busybody telephone operator was on duty that night. She listened in on calls she connected between your folks, and you know how she likes to gossip, even at that time of night.

"Yes, I can imagine. But what happened then? I asked.

"A major search was started. Some people in dune buggies went south on the beach. Others looked for you in boats on the Indian River. Traffic was heavy but slow as folks drove along South Indian River Drive beamin' powerful flashlights on the river shore.

"We felt real bad that we could not tell your families and the town that they had no cause to worry. But we were tryin' to protect you. About then, we received a telephone call from Rollie tellin' us that you had slipped away. We knew we had to find you before Cochrane did. Volunteers joined the deputies searchin' for you along the river between Palm City and Citrustown. Because of the rattlers, wild hogs and panthers out here, we had no idea that you would take off cross-country.

"Where did that airplane come from?" I asked the sheriff.

"Having heard that there was a search on, Herman Hersey offered his crop-duster plane," he replied. "I sent Hank to stand by with him at the airfield south of town. We were havin' no luck. About daybreak, Jake here took a call at the office from Sally's Uncle Andrew who said he saw Paul Cochrane pass his place on Okeechobee Road, and turn south on the Rim Ditch road. That's all we needed to know. Jake can tell you the rest."

"As the sheriff said, Hank was at the airfield waiting with Herman for daylight so that they could search from the air. Before we headed out this way, I phoned Hank and reported your Uncle Andrew's call. Hank tells me they took off in the plane and flew out here where Paul had been seen. In just a few minutes they spotted a car by the old lime pit, did a low fly-over, and saw two men struggling in the edge of the water with a girl nearby. They assumed the two men to be you and Cochrane.

"Yesterday, Herman had prepared his plane for a crop-dusting job. Knowing that fast action was necessary, Hank yelled to Herman to dust them and land. Banking around into the wind, Herman released a cloud of pesticide low over the lime pit, and set the plane down. Before the plane stopped rolling, Hank jumped out, and sprinted to the pit to save you, but you already had Cochrane pinned down. Both of you had a snoot full of the pesticide. It was easy for Hank to take Cochrane as we were driving up. We hope you don't have any ill effects from that bug dust. Sally must have got some, too."

"At the time, I thought I was dying," I said, "but I'm okay now. How about you, Sally?"

"I was so excited, I wouldn't know if I breathed any of it or not. But I feel no ill effects."

Before we could ask anymore questions, Jake turned on to Okeechobee Road and drove into Andrew Graham's front yard. Sally's Aunt Maggie was first out of the house, followed closely by Andrew. They greeted us excitedly as we got out of the car. "Glory be!" Maggie exclaimed as she hugged Sally. "We have been so worried. Where have you children been?"

"It's a long story, Aunt Maggie," Sally said.

CHAPTER 9

The sheriff went into the house with Andrew Graham to call his office. Making our way through the well-wishers, we followed and waited anxiously while he gave instructions to his dispatcher on the other end of the line.

Sally and I called our families letting them know that we were safe, and made arrangements to meet them at the courthouse. Aunt Maggie took Sally upstairs. Soon, Sally returned with her face washed and her hair combed. The blouse, shorts and sneakers she had on at Manatee Creek were a little muddy, but considering what she had been through, she looked terrific. A bright smile lit up her lovely golden face. What a girl! I thought.

Sally and I went out in the yard where I not too modestly accepted the plaudits of the small group congratulating us on our successful escape. As yet, I had not thought of a graceful way to tell them that we would have been better off if we had stayed where we were. In the crowd of well-wishers I spotted Harcord Ritchey.

"What are you doing out here, Harcord?" I asked.

Andrew Graham, having overheard my question, said, "He's the reason I saw Paul Cochrane drive by. Harcord was outside the sheriff's office when the call came that you and Sally had slipped away from the Fultz place. He overheard the sheriff discussing where you might be going. Remembering the stop you made here the other day, Harcord had a hunch that you might be coming to our place so he borrowed a car, drove out here, and knocked on our door just at sunrise. He told us that you kids were missing and might be out this way.

I got dressed and was letting Harcord in the house when we saw Paul Cochrane going by."

"That hunch probably saved our lives, my friend Harcord. You shall forever have my gratitude," I said, shaking his hand.

"Oh, it was nothin'. Just seems you always need lookin' after, that's all. Ain' nobody likes an adventure like you do."

Sally and I thanked her uncle and aunt for their part in rescuing us, and their hospitality. Jake started the Lincoln and we resumed our place in Sheriff Bogar's car. Jake had taken the convertible top down and we drove on Okeechobee Road heading a small motorcade going into Fort Capron. Somehow the news had spread that we were coming. People were shouting and waving as we passed and we waved back. This was getting to be fun. Upon approaching the courthouse, we were amazed to see hundreds of people on the west lawn. A cheer went up when we drove into a parking space reserved for us.

As we stepped down from the car, news reporters from Miami radio stations WIOD and WQAM stuck microphones in our faces firing questions. Sheriff Bo held them back with assurances that he would be holding a news conference. The sheriff was masterminding the proceedings. The breaking of this bootlegging and gambling ring was a feather in his ten-gallon hat, and he was making the most of it.

Sally and I pushed our way through the crowd to our families. Sally and Lil hugged each other, screamed and talked, all at the same time. Randy was there, as were Nell, Eddie, and Charles, all of them shouting questions at us and celebrating our safe return. Waiting patiently on the courthouse steps was my mother, smiling with tears in her eyes.

When I bent down to kiss Mother on the cheek, she whispered, "Welcome home, son." I asked her forgiveness for causing her so much worry. Sally joined us and Mother gave her a hug.

Parked in front of the jail next door was the federal

agents' car. It occurred to me that Paul Cochrane must be locked up over there, cursing his luck.

Much confusion ensued as the throng, including the reporters from the radio stations and the newspapers, crowded toward the courthouse entrance where chairs, bunting-draped rostrum, microphone, and loudspeaker had been hastily assembled. The news reporters scrambled for a good position. Jake Archer was directing us to our seats when Sally said, "Hey! There's Rollie!"

I looked where Sally was pointing, and saw our host of last night hanging back on the edge of the crowd smiling happily. Sally made her way back to Rollie, took his hand and brought him up to the front, and apologized for running away. Everybody laughed.

Sheriff Bo moved behind the rostrum, held up a big hand and the crowd quieted down. Speaking into the microphone, he said, "Good mornin', folks, and a real, good mornin' it is."

A cheer went up from the crowd. Continuing on, he said, "We're goin' to have us a news conference here, but first, I'd like to make a few remarks. I tried to tell you that guy Cochrane was no good when he ran against Joe last year, but most of you just wouldn't listen. I know a lot of you think politicians like Joe and me are scoundrels, but you got to realize how we play the game. Some things are more serious than others. We sometimes let the little things go; maybe we do a few favors now and then. However, when we see somethin' that might hurt the folks of our county that we love so much, we get serious and try to do somethin' about it."

"Tell us about the kids. Who took them and how did they get free?" the reporter from WQAM yelled.

"Just hold your horses and let me finish," the sheriff answered. "I'll get around to that in a minute."

"Our eyes were opened during that last campaign. A lot of money was spent by Cochrane, and after the election, I started doin' some checkin' around to find where the money was comin' from and why. Lately, I ain't been too excited by a little bootleggin', Prohibition bein' about over. But when someone uses our unguarded beaches for major fund-raisin' to finance a power takeover, I get interested. Cochrane was plannin' to buy his way to the governor's chair at the next general election.

"We knew we could get him for bootleggin', but we needed more than that to really put him away. These young people—you all know Scotty, and his girlfriend, Sally Graham, from Atlanta—who are about as adventuresome as they are brave and smart, gave us the chance we had been lookin' for. They did not know it at first, but they actually witnessed a murder Cochrane committed. Later they suspected that there might have been a murder, and cooked up a plan to try to verify it by looking for an anchor that was missing from a line tied around the victim. Thinkin' that Cochrane was a good guy, and bein' suspicious of me, they reported to him everything they were doing. That's how Cochrane concluded that they had witnessed the murder, and would eventually tie him to it. He could not let them live. Now, I'll take your questions."

"Did they find an anchor?" a reporter from the local paper asked.

"Yes, and we saw them do it because Jake Archer and Hank Slade had Scotty and Sally under surveillance at Manatee Creek. When they found the anchor that was the clue to the murder, Jake and Hank picked them up without telling them it was for their protection, because we were still trying to smoke out Cochrane. When Scotty and Sally got away, they were in great danger. We had to find them before Cochrane did.

"You folks will know eventually how close this all came to bein' a real tragedy. It didn't because this town came alive at midnight last night. Betty Foster, our central telephone operator, did what she always has done when she learns that something important has happened that you ought to know about. She heard that the young people were missing, and took it upon herself to wake up some of you to spread the alarm, which started the biggest search this town has ever seen."

"Why didn't you tell us you had them when the town started looking for them?" a voice in the crowd asked.

"It probably was a mistake, but we were trying to smoke out Cochrane. Once we lost 'em ourselves, we were searching with you. One man had sense enough to figure out that Scott and Sally had gone out to Five Mile. That man is Harcord Ritchey. He deserves a lot of credit for makin' this thing turn out the way it did."

I was glad to hear Harcord getting the recognition for what he did. The sheriff continued," Richey and Sally's Uncle Andrew saw Cochrane out there at sunrise and called us. Jake Archer called Hank Slade, who was standing by with Herman Hersey and his crop-dusting plane. They flew out there and saved the kids who Cochrane was planning to kill."

"How did they save them?" a reporter asked.

"You won't believe this, but Herman disabled Cochrane by showering him with pesticide when he and Scott were struggling in a lime pit. They landed the plane, and Hank took over from there. If Harcord Ritchey had not thought to go to Five Mile, you all can guess what would have happened to Scott and Sally. I want to publicly thank Harcord and Betty Foster, and especially the people of this county for showing how much they care when young people are in trouble. That's about all from me. Now let's hear from two great youngsters that you should be proud of."

Sheriff Bogar stepped back as Sally and I rose, walked to the rostrum, and stood there hand in hand amidst the cheers and applause of the crowd. Eventually, the applause died down and Sally whispered to me to do the talking.

"Friends," I began, "thank you very much. You will have to pardon me for the way I look, but Sally looks great, doesn't she?" Another cheer went up for Sally, smiling broadly, and she graciously accepted the plaudits of the crowd.

"As you have heard, I had a lime pit mud bath a little while ago. Because of you, I'm not in that lime pit now with a bullet in my head. You are treating us like heroes. Sally Graham is a hero, but I am not; I'm just plain stupid. I owe the sheriff an apology. All those times I saw him leaning back in the chair outside his office looking half-asleep, I thought he wasn't much interested in anything but getting reelected. Now, it appears that he was sitting there keeping an eye on things and thinking about doing the job he is elected to do, and doing it his way.

"When it really mattered, I didn't trust him. I trusted a young, smart politician that I didn't know all that well. I nearly messed up the sheriff's investigation; I jeopardized the safety of someone I've grown to admire and care for a lot, and I nearly got myself killed. If that isn't stupid, I don't know what is.

"Sally joins me in thanking all of you for all that you did for us. In addition to Sheriff Bo, Jake Archer, Deputy Hank Slade, and Herman Hersey, we want to especially thank my friend, Harcord Ritchie, for having the good sense to figure out where we might be.

"That's about all I have to say. It's nice to be alive this morning. Sally and I love you all." We waved to the cheers of the wonderful people of Fort Capron gathered there for us, and stepped down from the rostrum, letting a beaming Sheriff Bogart conclude the proceedings. After answering questions from the press and radio reporters, Sally and I were ready to go home for some sleep. Charlie and Eddie told us that it would be party time at the hotel tonight. We said we would be there, but for now, we were leaving with our families for some much needed rest.

The celebration renewed at the Saturday Summer Night Dance in the Terrace Room of the hotel. I had slept most of the day, and after supper drove to the Grahams' for Sally. We were a little late getting to the hotel and by the time we arrived the dance was in full swing. As we walked through the door, the dance music stopped, and Gus' band broke into "Happy Days Are Here Again." Eddie and Charlie led the young crowd in singing the good news song with enthusiasm. Embarrassed somewhat, but nonetheless enjoying it, we joined the dancing when the band resumed with the melodic and appropriate, "Can This Be Love?"

During a break in the music, a group cornered us, wanting to know firsthand of our experience.

"Hey, you guys are famous, and from what I heard on the WQAM radio news at six tonight, you had quite a night! Tell us about it," Charles said.

"Well, it was kind of exciting," I replied. "We were bewildered, and sometime downright scared, especially towards the last. The snakes, alligators, and panthers weren't so bad, but all joking aside, that Paul Cochrane was going to kill us." By then we were asked to come to the front, where all could hear, and proceeded to relate the story of our abduction and escape.

Eventually, Sally and I had said about all we could say, and answered questions as best we could. The music and dancing resumed and, wanting to be alone, we quietly slipped out of the Terrace Room and walked out on the dock.

Sally earlier had mentioned that there was something she wanted to tell me. We walked out to the end of the dock. No moon was shining but the stars were bright, and a soft sea breeze cooled the late summer evening.

I turned to Sally, gathered her in my arms, and asked, "Now, what is it you wanted to tell me?"

"Let's go over and sit on the bench. I can't think straight when you hold me like that."

"Well, here we are on the bench, and I am only holding your hand. What is this that seems so important?"

"Darling, I am going home tomorrow. Today, I talked to Mother and John—he's the boy I'm engaged to marry. I phoned Mother, telling her of our experience. She, of course, called John, and he phoned me. They are both worried about me, and anxious for me to return. I have been here longer than I originally planned because of you."

"But I can't let you go. I love you. We are perfect for each other. You can't get married. You love me."

"Oh, Scott, you make it sound so wonderful. But this has all happened so fast. I need time to sort things out—and so do you. You have your plans for college, and you want to be a journalist some day; a day that is a long time off. I would just be in your way. We shouldn't do anything that either of us will regret."

Nothing I said could make Sally change her mind. She was right, of course, but, I was desperately afraid of losing her. However, if after she returned to Atlanta, she decided to marry John, I never really had her after all. In ten days, I will be going to Marietta. Perhaps by then I will know.

Sally was to leave for Atlanta on the three o'clock train the next afternoon. In the morning, I went with her to the Presbyterian church which all the Grahams attend. Afterwards, we had dinner at our house. My mother had become very fond of Sally, and she wanted to see Sally one last time. With us for the noon meal was Mrs. Brigitta Konreid, a wealthy widow who had a big house down the river. She seemed very interested in Sally.

After dinner, Mrs. Konreid asked Sally, "Young lady, are you going to college?"

"Oh, no,, ma'am," Sally replied. "My family's situation is such that it just isn't possible. Besides, there are plans made in Atlanta that rule out college for me."

"That does seem a shame. You're a very bright girl, and I understand you are a tennis champion," Mrs. Konreid said.

"You are very kind, Mrs. Konreid, and, yes, I did play tennis rather well in high school."

It was time for us to leave. Sally turned to Mother and said, "Mrs. Forrester, thank you for inviting me to dinner. Everything was delicious. I must be going now as I have some last minute packing yet to do but I'm most grateful for your warm hospitality. I'm sorry we caused you and Mr. Forrester so much worry and trouble, but these few weeks in Fort Capron will be a time I shall never forget."

After a hug from Mother and a handshake from Dad, we drove to Lil's house for the last time. Sally sat very close to me. I didn't look at her, but I think she was crying.

The many friends Sally had made during her visit were at the Florida East Coast Railway station to see her off. Sally gave me as much time as she could, and I laughed and joked with the others, but my heart wasn't in it. All too soon, a whistle sounded signaling the arrival of the three o'clock train, right on time. The big steam engine came puffing and wheezing by, and rumbled slowly to a stop, accompanied by the sound of screeching brakes and escaping steam.

Spotting the number of Sally's car, we all hurried along the station amidst shouted good-byes. I gave Sally's bags to a porter and stood back, waiting while she hugged her many relatives and friends. As the "all aboard" was shouted by the conductor, she turned and kissed me, whispering in my ear, "Don't phone or write but please call me when you get to Marietta." She disappeared into the Pullman car.

My heart pounded in time with the chugs of the steam

engine pulling the train from the station. Was this the last I would ever see of Sally? I wondered what the future held for us.

CHAPTER 10

Mother and Dad had not gone to the railroad station. Returning home, I found them reading the Sunday edition of the Miami Herald with an Associated Press article relating to our abduction and rescue. Surely this account would make the Atlanta Journal and I chuckled to myself thinking of fiancée John's reaction when he reads of the night Sally and I spent together.

"Mom, it was nice having Mrs. Konreid here for dinner, but she hasn't joined us for dinner after church before. Was there any special reason why she was here today?" I asked.

"Brigitta called last evening wanting to know if there were some way she might visit with Sally. Since we were having Sally for dinner, I suggested that Mrs. Konreid join us after services."

"Mrs. Konreid did show an interest in Sally. I wonder why?" I said.

"It may have something to do with Rollins College in Winter Park. She is a member of the Board of Trustees. Rollins is a good liberal arts college, but the tuition is rather high. Most of the students are from well-to-do families. I doubt if Sally could enroll there," Mother said. "Besides, apparently Sally has other plans."

"That's just it, Mom, Sally did have other plans before she came to Fort Capron. She's supposedly engaged to a fellow she has known since the Grahams moved to Atlanta. She's never gone out with anyone else and it's always been assumed that he and Sally would marry. Things have changed since she went to Bank Night with me. Bank Night, for gosh sakes—what a way to start a new romance! Anyway, now she's not so sure. She's going home to try to sort things out. I'm to call her when I get to Marietta."

"What a tangled web you have woven for yourself, son. But isn't she young to be getting married?"

"She'll soon be nineteen. She lost a year in school when they moved to Atlanta from North Carolina. Many girls get married when they are nineteen years old. She knows how I feel about her, but I realize that ours has not been a normal romance. I can't expect her to be sure of the way she feels until she has the opportunity to view our relationship, unclouded by sharks, gators, snakes, panthers, abductions, murder, and me. I'm in no position to ask her to marry me, but I don't want her to marry somebody else either."

"You'll have to wait and see what happens. In the meantime, you must finish up at the lumberyard and go to freshman orientation at the university. I suggest that you run upstairs and get some rest. Now that the excitement is over, you look tired," Mother said, worrying about my welfare as usual.

I did as she said, and climbed between the cool sheets of a freshly made bed. The next I knew, I had slept the clock around, the alarm startling me awake at 6:30 in the morning. My first thought was of Sally. After a change in Jacksonville, her train should be arriving in Atlanta. How glorious the last forty-eight hours have been! But my celebrity status had ended; it was time to go back to work.

My first assignment for the day was a delivery to the Fords, who were remodeling their old house on the south side of town. As I pulled into their driveway, the men working on the job came over and could talk about nothing but my weekend experience. They wanted to know how it felt to wrestle for my life, and some were quick to tell me how they joined in the search for us. Apparently, I continued to remain a celebrity of sorts.

Eventually the truck was unloaded, and the men got on with their remodeling. On the way back to the yard, I stopped by Stoddards' to see what, if anything, Eddie had decided about going to college. We had not had a chance to discuss it at the celebration Saturday night. After parking the truck, I approached Eddie where he was cleaning a customer's windshield and asked him what his plans were.

Eddie put his sponge in a bucket and replied, "With the help of Mr. Homer at school, I did some checking, and have made up my mind to give it a try. I told Ma that I would take no more than one hundred dollars of her Bank Night money. With that, I can pay the registration fee, buy the first books I'll need, and have about fifty dollars left over. Mr. Homer has helped me send a campus job application to the university with his endorsement as principal of our high school. I need a job that will pay enough to cover my meals and help with the cost of a room in the dorm. With that, and any other employment I can find, I can go and stay as long as that fifty dollars will last."

"That's great!" I said. "Drive up to freshman orientation with me this weekend. I was going Friday afternoon, but if we leave on Thursday, you can spend all day Friday pushing your application through the system."

Eddie finished serving the customer and rang up the payment at the cash register inside. There being no other customers waiting at the gas pumps, Eddie climbed on a stool and took a swig on a Coke he had pulled out of the cold drink box, and said, "That might help. Mr. Homer was afraid that all the jobs may be filled. I certainly would appreciate the opportunity to meet those folks face-to-face. Mr. Homer has the name of the employment officer. I could even look around for something else to earn a few bucks of cash money each week. Mr. Stoddard is giving me every encouragement; a letter of recommendation from him went up with the application. So I feel sure that he'll let me off."

"Okay, then. We can work Thursday morning as usual, then leave in the afternoon. I'll pick you up at your house at one and we should be in Gainesville by five. We'll have to get a room somewhere Thursday night, but I have my dorm room assignment and maybe they will let us use that room the rest of the weekend. So, here we go, Eddie! Hopefully, we're going to be a couple of Gators together."

Dad called me into his office when I got back to the yard. After discussing the delivery to the Fords, leaning back in the swivel chair behind his big desk, he said, "I've made a decision about your replacement when you finish this week. I will take Harcord on as a full-time employee if he wants the job. "

"Great news," I said. "It's good for him, and it's good for you. Nobody will work harder and be more dependable."

"I've been watching him. Harcord's not only a hard worker and dependable, he's smart. When we were all in a panic the other night, accomplishing nothing, he's the one that thought the situation through and figured which way you and Sally would most likely be going. I can see him as yard foreman here some day."

I nodded when my father suggested Harcord becoming the foreman, but he held up his hand, turned his chair, looked out a window, and said reflectively, "However, that could present a problem with some of the yard-men being white, and Harcord colored. I don't know if the whites would like taking orders from a colored man. It's a shame. Maybe the day will come when a man will be judged by how hard he works, or how smart he is, and not by the color of his skin."

"Dad, you and Mother have made clear to me the injustices you see every day, and your inability to do much about them. It could be that this is what has made me want to be a journalist."

"In the matter of influence, it has been said that the pen is a mighty weapon. But it should be used to build up, not pull down. The world is full of fault-finders. Don't add to the list when you feel the urge to be judgmental."

"I'll try to remember that. But, about Harcord—he knows what he's up against. He'll stand up for his right to be respected, but in a way that'll get results."

"Well, for now we must find out if he wants to work here full-time. I would appreciate it if you would get in touch with him, and ask him to come see me. Your time with us will soon end, and, if Harcord will take my offer, I want him to start right away."

"I'll call his mother. If he's working somewhere today, she'll give him the message. Dad, I would like my time here to end a day sooner than planned. Eddie Russell has decided to go to the university. He's accepting just enough of his mother's Bank Night money to get started and has applied for a campus job that he must have in order to stay there. It might help if, when we go up for orientation, we got to Gainesville Thursday, and that would give Eddie all day Friday to follow up on the application. I'm asking if I could leave at noon Thursday."

"Certainly you can, son. Eddie is a fine young man, and he's energetic and intelligent. If a reference from me would do any good, I'd be glad to give one."

We discussed the transition of my work to Harcord, and the plans for the Marietta visit. I called Mrs. Ritchey at work and she said Harcord was planting an orange grove in the backcountry.

"Please tell Harcord that my father wants to see him about working for him regularly," I said.

"I certainly will, Mr. Jeff, and he'll be mighty pleased to hear that. I'll tell him as soon as he comes home this evenin'."

While I was looking for the imaginary treasure last week, more stock for the paint store had come which had to be removed from cartons and put away on the shelves. I was busy doing this job when Hank Slade came in.

"Howdy, Hank," I said, "It's good to see you. I'm glad you came by because I've never had a chance to properly thank you for what you did the other morning. I thought I was a goner before you blinded Paul with that pesticide. The whole experience seems like a dream. From the time you made Sally and me get in that boat cabin, until you saved us, I was on an adrenaline high. It was difficult to come down off of it."

"You looked like you were winnin' the battle of the lime pit by the time I got there. At the beginning, I was just as confused as you were and I still wonder why Bo couldn't let you and me know what was going on. He had his reasons, I guess. He sent me over here to ask you to go see him when you can."

"If it is real important I can go anytime, but if it can wait I would like to make it Wednesday. People have been stopping by all afternoon to talk about Friday night. It's difficult to get things done. After I finish with this paint, I have another delivery to make that's being loaded on the truck right now. Tomorrow looks like it will be the same."

"I'll tell Bo that you suggested Wednesday. If there's a problem, I'll call you back," Hank said as he left. I finished putting up the paint, and made a delivery of roofing material out on Okeechobee Road. It was 6:30 by the time I returned to the yard and went home.

While I was busy I didn't have time to think much about Sally, but after supper while I was sitting in the gazebo on the river's bluff in front of our house, I felt her presence. Perhaps it was the evening breeze and our happy hours together that reminded me of her. I remembered the last time we sat there watching the moon rise over the island across the way. In repose, her face framed by curly brown hair, Sally's hazel eyes were calm reflecting a special beauty that shone from within.

But Sally wasn't there; she was in Atlanta deciding what she was going to do about John. I had to suffer the wait until I got to Marietta. In the meantime, there was work to finish, the sheriff to see, and arrangements to be made for the trips to Gainesville and Georgia. I would just have to get on with it.

CHAPTER 11

When we had lunch at Stoddard's on Tuesday, Eddie said that he would very much like a reference from my father. He said he would pick it up before we left so he could thank him personally. Nell Stone's sister was taking her back home to Perry, Georgia the next morning and would be having a farewell party for Nell that night.

"You're coming to the party for Nell, aren't you?" Eddie asked.

"I wouldn't miss it," I replied. "Misery loves company, and I want to see if you'll be as miserable as I've been since Sally left."

"Nell is a lot of fun, and I am glad that she'll be a freshman at South Georgia College in Douglas so we can see more of each other, but we're not as serious as you and Sally appear to be. You might have to look elsewhere to find someone as miserable as you."

Getting up to leave, I said, "I'll see you at the party, and if there're any last minute plans to be made we can discuss them then."

When I got back to the lumberyard, I found Harcord in the paint store rearranging the stock. Sneaking up behind him, I said, "Hey, man! What are you doing up on that ladder?"

"Don't interrupt me. I've got to straighten out this mess. The guy I'm replacin' has got the varnish with the house paint. Mr. Forrester said I'd find things like this. I told him not to worry, it will all be in order soon," Harcord said, turning around and acting surprised. "Oh, hey, Scotty. I didn't know that was you."

"What a fib," I said. "It looks like you've seen Dad, and this place will have to struggle along the best it can with you."

"Seriously, this is the chance I have been waiting for. You can't appreciate how good it will feel to wake up in the morning and know that I have a steady job. That father of yours is one fine man. There are plenty of white men standing in line for this job, but he chose me. I'll try hard to make certain he never regrets it."

I assured Harcord of Dad's confidence in him, and told him how glad I was that I could go off to college knowing that my good friend was where he wanted to be, just as I would be where I wanted to be.

The farewell party for Nell was a lively one. She had visited Fort Capron before and would return, but this was an excuse to have another get-together before the summer ended. Most of the conversation was of the happy high school years which had come to an end, and the plans of those fortunate enough to be going off to college. Eddie was acting confident about his chances of getting the job and making it at the university, at least for the first year. He even invited Nell down to Gainesville as his date for Fall Frolics.

Fall Frolics was the first big dance weekend at the university when the last football game of the year was played. We had heard that Glen Gray's orchestra was to provide the music. I wistfully wondered if Sally would be free to accept an invitation from me. The first game of the year would be in Gainesville with Stetson University soon after school opened.

Early Wednesday morning was devoted to showing Harcord the routine for opening up the yard. He was going to be doing more than just loading and unloading lumber. I left him looking after the paint and hardware store when I went to see Sheriff Bo. The greeting I received was much different than when I was reporting on the bootlegging. Jake was not there, but Hank was on duty. He told me to go on in, that the sheriff was expecting me.

"Good morning, Scotty," the sheriff said, leaning back in a chair with his feet on his desk. "Thank you for comin' in. I guess you've had some difficulty settlin' down. I know I have. Seems like people won't let you be. There was a reporter from the Miami Herald wantin' to interview you. I told her I would check with you and get back to her. Just what are you going to be doing between now and when you leave for college?"

"The plans are pretty well set. Eddie Russell and I are going up to Gainesville for freshman orientation this weekend, and then I'll be leaving on Tuesday for Marietta to visit my sister Harriet for a couple of weeks. I don't see how I can have time for that Miami Herald interview. There's not anything I could tell her that she doesn't already know."

"It's a lady reporter. I think she's interested in what might be a love angle between you and Sally."

"That settles it! Please tell her that I'll be out of town and unavailable for an interview. The situation between Sally and me is kind of up in the air right now, and the last person I would want to discuss it with is a reporter."

"I'll take care of it. But that's not why I wanted to talk to you. Paul Cochrane, bankin' on a plea bargain, has made a confession of sorts and told us a lot about his gamblin' operation and some of the people involved, but we don't believe that he has told us everything, and we may need your help."

Hearing that remark gave me a sinking sensation. I'd had enough of dealing with the Paul Cochrane situation and said, "I will help you in any way I reasonably can, but I was sort of hoping this was all wrapped up and that I could get on with my life."

The sheriff took his feet off the desk and turning, faced me saying, "I can certainly understand that but I feel like I got an itch I can't scratch. Cochrane has given us the names of some guys from other counties, but nobody local. We just don't see how he could have put this all together without some major help from around here, and I don't mean just some foot soldiers. I'm talkin' about serious support from somebody wantin' power."

That surprised me. I'd always been under the impression that nobody knew more about what's happening in this county than he did and I told him so.

"I thought so, too, but sometimes a person can know so much he overlooks the obvious. My problem is that we can't account for everybody that should have been on the beach that night. If I remember right, you said it was some shoutin' you heard that attracted your attention to the boat landing on the beach."

"Yes. It was the yelling that made us look down that way."

"That's what I wanted to ask you about. I know you don't know who was doin' the yellin' or you would have told me, but do you think you would recognize the voice if you heard it again?"

"Oh, I don't know. Maybe I could, but I doubt it."

"Well, we would appreciate it if you could give that some thought, and keep your ears open as you go around town. If there is someone else locally who might have been involved, it'll be somebody we wouldn't expect."

I told the sheriff that I would do that, and if I thought of anything else that might be helpful, I would let him know. I reminded him that next week I'd be in Marietta, and if he needed me for anything, he could get Harriet's telephone number from Mother. On the way out, I thanked Hank again for his part in our rescue, and asked him to express my appreciation to Herman Hersey for his help if I didn't get a chance to tell him myself.

I didn't get much work done Thursday morning. Most of Dad's employees had been with him for years, and some I had known since I was just a youngster. They had been very helpful to me, and I went to each expressing my appreciation. I was touched when they presented me with a baby gator, mounted by a taxidermist.

Although I had worked in the yard from time to time in the past, this was my first period of regular employment. It was a good experience because it gave me a taste of what the retail lumber and hardware business is really like. While I had not found it especially appealing, it did provide me something against which to compare other endeavors, such as journalism. Dad had a good and honorable business and one of us should follow in his footsteps. Anyway, from what he paid me, I was able to put away a little money which will come in handy this year in college.

CHAPTER 12

Eddie was waiting when I arrived at his house after lunch. We would be gone only three nights, so there was room in the rumble seat for our small amount of luggage. Mrs. Russell was smiling broadly as we left, proud to see her son going off to prepare for college.

Like two young knights leaving home to conquer the world, Eddie and I rode up U.S. 1, turned across the state at Indian River City, drove through Orlando and on up to Gainesville.

Summer school still being in session, we went to the Student Center, which had an information desk where we could ask about overnight housing on or near the campus. We were told to telephone Ma Pritchard's Rooming House which, during the regular school year, housed only students from the law school, but that Mrs. Pritchard might let us have a room for the night. I remembered that my brother-in-law, Edward Wilson, who was married to my sister Mary, had roomed there when he was in law school. I phoned Mrs. Pritchard, and when I told her who I was, she agreed to let us have a room for the night for two dollars that included a bath and linens. When we checked in, she recommended The College Inn for supper, and Piggy Park for breakfast.

We found that The College Inn was not actually an inn, it was just an eating place convenient to the campus with booths against the wall and tables in the middle. The summer session was coming to an end, and from the conversations in the restaurant it appeared that the students were cramming for final exams. We found a booth where our naivete would not be so noticeable.

After supper, Eddie and I went back to the Student Center and learned that the offices we would be looking for the next day were in the administration building located in the northeast corner of the campus. Shooting pool in the Student Center recreation room, we met other incoming freshman who had arrived early for orientation. Seeing students walking through the building, carrying books, talking and laughing, and sitting in the lounge reading, instilled in us our first taste of college life. We returned to Ma Pritchard's and retired for the night, setting a travel alarm clock for an early rising.

Piggy Park was a large diner with thirty stools lined up along the counter. Two girls took orders and shouted them in a language of their own to the cook in the small kitchen. The name is inspired by the specialty of the diner, which is a foot-long pork hot dog served on a sesame seed bun topped by a mound of hot sauerkraut. The specialty did not appeal to me for breakfast, so I ordered scrambled eggs with ham and grits. Eddie couldn't resist; he ordered the hot dog.

After breakfast, we headed for the administration building, which was near Piggy Park. Eddie and I were waiting at the entrance when the building opened at 8:30. A receptionist directed Eddie to the campus employment office, and me to an office where I could confirm my dormitory room assignment. Eddie's need to know about a job was the more important so I decided to go with him to the employment office.

Standing at a file cabinet with her back to us was a woman in the process of removing a file. Turning around, she saw us standing there, and said, "Good morning, boys, what can I do for you?" She was very efficient looking, and seemed eager to help us.

"My name is Edgar Russell. You should have received my application for a job. Mr. Homer, my principal from San

Lucia High, helped me send it in about a week ago. I need some work if I'm going to be able to go to college. I also have another reference here." He handed her the letter Dad had written.

"My name is Ann Jones, Edgar. As a matter of fact, I have your file on my desk and have been trying to find something for you. The application came in so late that most of the jobs are gone. You have excellent references, and certainly have shown a need."

"It came in late, because until two weeks ago, I had no idea that I could go to college. My mother won some money at Bank Night in Fort Capron, and I have accepted one hundred dollars from her. She wants so much for me to go to college, and so do I. If you could just find me a job, you would make my mom and me both very happy."

Eddie was turning on the charm of which he had so much. I thought he was overdoing the sympathy angle a little more than necessary, but it appeared to be working. Ann Jones was smiling. She wasn't a bad-looking lady, and not long out of college herself.

"Something did turn up yesterday. A boy called and said he wouldn't want the job we had given him. Apparently he didn't like the hours."

"I'll take it, no matter what it is," Eddie said.

"You better be an early riser because the job is in the cafeteria kitchen as an assistant cook. You'll have to be at the cafeteria at six each morning to start making doughnuts, but you'll be out of there before ten. In the evening, your hours will be from five to eight. Don't tell me you can't cook, because I don't want to hear it. The pay is twenty-five cents an hour, and you get your meals free."

"Miss Jones, you've got yourself an expert doughnut maker. When do I start?"

"You start after you register in September. Come by here

first, and I'll give you a slip that will be honored when the registrar's office is making your class assignments. To complete this, I have some paperwork to do. Come back in about two hours, and I'll have the contract for your signature."

"Ma'am, I certainly do thank you for this opportunity. This is my friend, Scott Forrester. He'll be a freshman this year, and we are going to the residence office to see if maybe we can room together. His daddy wrote that last letter."

"The residence office is on the second floor. Good luck to you boys. Let me know if I can help you."

As we left, Eddie said, "This was a good idea to come today. We get to know some of these fine people, and learn our way around. That job will take care of my meals and provide money to pay my dormitory fee."

"Yeh, but you're going to have to get up at 5:30 every morning. Man, that's early!"

"I'll just have to do it. Now, let's go to that residence office."

We found the office upstairs and walked in. Some of the guys we saw at the Student Center last night were there. I gave a receptionist my name. She said she would call me when my turn came up. We found chairs and chatted with the others were who were waiting. They were from all over the state, places we'd never heard of, like one was from Okahumpka, and another from Quincy, which we learned was out in the panhandle of Florida. Okahumpka is near Leesburg in Lake County. The Quincy boy's family grows tobacco, and in Okahumpka they grow watermelons.

Quincy and Okahumpka went in before us, coming out shortly to tell us that their rooms were in Thomas Hall, which they said was one of the new dormitories. We went into an inner office when our names were called and were greeted by a man named Charles Parker. He checked down the list of room assignments and found that I was scheduled for Thomas

Hall. I introduced him to Eddie and told him about Eddie's recent decision to go to college and asked if we could room together. Mr. Parker said that a student from Tampa had been advised that he and I were rooming together.

"Mr. Parker, isn't there anything you can do about that? Eddie and I are best friends." I pleaded.

"The university's policy is to keep the same assignment unless both students agree to switch. At this late date, it would be impractical to ask the Tampa boy to accept some other room now that he has been notified. I'll tell you what I could do. There are rooms in Buckman Hall that have not been filled in which I could put you, but I warn you that Buckman Hall is the oldest dormitory on campus and the accommodations leave a little to be desired."

I turned to Eddie. "How does that sound to you?"

"It sounds fine to me, but you shouldn't take an old room when you could have a new one. I'll be happy with whoever turns out to be my roommate."

"No, sir, we are going to room together. A room's a room. That dorm couldn't be too bad, or the school wouldn't be using it. It's settled then. Since this is the only dorm where we can room together, we'll take a room in Buckman Hall."

"If you can put up with old furniture and facilities, you may learn to like Buckman Hall," Parker said. "It's well located, and has developed a nobility that comes with old age. There are seniors in Buckman Hall who would live nowhere else."

I asked Mr. Parker if we could see the room and stay there tonight. He got up from his desk, opened a cabinet, and took out a key.

"If you boys sign the residence agreement and pay the dorm deposit, you can have the key and look at the room, but you must bring it back this afternoon before five; occupancy is not permitted until school starts."

Mr. Parker pulled a form from his desk, filled in our names and the room number, and we signed it. I gave him a check for the deposit on my account in the San Lucia Bank. Eddie wanted to pay his share on the spot, but I told him we could make the adjustment when we paid the dormitory fee.

We thanked Mr. Parker for his help, and he gave us the key and a campus map showing the location of Buckman Hall. We could see that it was on the west side of the campus across the street from the Student Center.

I had left my car near Piggy Park. It was mid-morning so we stopped by the diner to have a Coke. The girls weren't busy, and we struck up a conversation. One was obviously older than the other. They could tell that we would be freshmen, because we acted a little big for our britches.

"Well fellows, you're leavin' home and goin' to be college boys," the older one said. "I've been workin' this diner for fifteen years, and you look just like the rest of them did when they were startin' out, but it don't take long to see that some has got it and others don't. You can have a good time here, yet if that's all you're interested in, you better go back home."

The younger counter girl was smiling as she said, "Boys, that's the speech Maude makes to all the freshmen she comes across. It may sound corny, but she speaks the truth. And I'm telling you that you can't make any better friend around here than Maude. She knows more about what's going on than anyone, and that includes the president, Dr. John Tigert."

As we were getting up to leave, Eddie turned on his charm and said, "Her name's Maude. What's your name?"

"Why, honey, my name's Annie. What's yours?"

"You two cut that out," Maude said. "It's plain to see that these boys has got a lot to do to get settled in."

"Don't worry, Miss Maude. Much as I would like to, I won't be over this way often. I just got a job working at the cafeteria, and get most of my pay in eating my meals there. My pal, Scotty, maybe will be around. He won't have to eat in the cafeteria. Scotty's going to need help because he's in love and scared another guy is going to get his girl. But, I'd surely like you two to be my friends so if I need some sisterly, or, pardon the expression, motherly advice, I'll know where to come to get it. By the way, my name's Eddie."

I nudged Eddie in the ribs for referring to my situation with Sally, even though what he said was accurate. Annie took our money and we left, going first to ask Mrs. Pritchard to let us stay tonight. She agreed, and with the campus map in hand, we went to find the place we would be living for months, or maybe years, to come.

The campus map showed Buckman Hall in the center of much of the extracurricular activity at the university. Across the street was the building housing the Student Center, the cafeteria, and the student publications office. The intramural athletic department was in the new gymnasium next door where the college basketball games are played and big dances held. The football stadium was just a short walk away.

The stone walls of the exterior of Buckman Hall probably looked much as they did when built except that they were vine-clad, giving the old building a distinguished appearance. Entering the main hall through the front door, we saw the worn wooden floors and plaster walls wainscoted with dark-stained oak paneling. Shiny banisters of heavy oak bordered the well-trodden stairs leading to the upper floors.

Our room was on a corner with a view of the gymnasium on one side and the stadium on the other. There being only basic furniture, we would need to bring accessories from home to make our new habitat livable. The size of the room dictated the use of steel-framed bunk beds rather than single beds.

Being unselfish, Eddie volunteered to take the upper bunk. I gave that some thought, and remembering our schedules said, "No, thanks. I'll take the upper and you can have the lower. I don't care to have you step on me when you get up to make doughnuts at six in the morning."

The bath area, with showers, wash basins, and commodes, was communal with the occupants of three other rooms in our section of the second floor. All in all, we were very well satisfied with our decision to go for Buckman, even though it was old. Hopefully, the plumbing was not too old.

After lunch in the cafeteria, we set out to find a job for Eddie to supplement his income. We decided to go back to the campus employment office, and talk to Ann Jones. She was not busy when we got there and could see us right away.

"Miss Jones," Eddie said, "I know off-campus jobs aren't part of your duties, but do you have any suggestions as to where I might apply for a few hours of extra work a week?"

"Certain jobs can be fit into a student's schedule better than others," she replied. "To avoid class conflicts, night jobs are best, and they shouldn't be too time-consuming. You must have some time to study outside of class, you know. You might try bell-hopping in the Hotel Thomas, ticket-taking and ushering in the movie theater, or picking up laundry and dry cleaning."

"What about service-station work? I do that at home."

"Service-stations don't stay open very late here. They're busy only during the daytime."

We discussed the job situation a little longer and left for the Hotel Thomas. The manager tried to be helpful but made it clear that the only time he would need any extra help was on football weekends. Eddie wanted steadier work than that, so next we went to the only movie theater in Gainesville. "The Private Life of Henry the Eighth," with Charles Laughton playing King Henry was showing, but we were more interested in seeing the manager, not the movie. The manager there had all the help he needed and job applicants on a waiting list. At University Laundry a man by the name of Strickland was in charge. Eddie introduced himself, saying he needed to make some more money to stay in school.

Mr. Strickland explained that he did have students picking up and delivering laundry and dry cleaning around the campus at night for one-half of the charge ticket, with the student paying for the operation of his car, which he must have.

"Well, that does it for me," Eddie said. "I have no car."

I took Eddie aside and, over his objection, convinced him to use my car until he could make enough to get one of his own.

Eddie said, "My friend here tells me I can use his car until I get one of my own, so Mr. Strickland, I'd like to take a crack at any route you might have open."

"The better routes, like working the fraternity houses and the newer dorms, are taken, but I'll have a route in the swamps that will be open when school starts. You can have that one, if you think you can handle it."

"What are the swamps?" Eddie asked.

"Oh, that's what the students call the area north of University Avenue where the rooming and boarding houses are. About twenty per cent of the student body lives in the swamps. If you hustle, and the boys there like you, you can get enough business to make it worthwhile," Mr. Strickland said.

"Then I will do it. Save that route, and tell me when to start."

"The boys will come to college with clean clothes, so there is no need to begin until about ten days after you get here. But check in with me as soon as you arrive so I can know that the route is covered."

Eddie gave his name and home address, as well as his

campus address. We left the laundry feeling that we had accomplished this day what we had set out to do.

After dinner in the cafeteria, we went to the movie theater and saw Charles Laughton give the brilliant performance that had won him the Academy Award earlier in the year.

In the morning, we breakfasted with our friends at Piggy Park, and joined nearly a thousand other freshmen in the university auditorium for orientation.

President Tigert seemed warm and genuinely interested in the students as he welcomed us and stressed the scholastic and cultural opportunities at the University of Florida. The dean of students reviewed school traditions and student government with its executive council and honor court. Coach Bachman introduced some of his stars from last year's team, and a senior from the athletic council explained the operation of the intramural athletic program.

The incoming president of the sophomore class told what would be expected of us as Florida freshmen. Among other things, we were expected to wear little orange caps, known as rat caps, at all times when we were outside. The afternoon was set aside for a campus tour. Since we were fairly familiar with the campus, Eddie and I decided to skip the tour and go home.

CHAPTER 13

After an uneventful trip back to Fort Capron, I dropped Eddie off at his house in time for supper. The enthusiasm with which he related the events of our visit to the university brought tears to his proud mother's eyes. There was no doubt in my mind that Eddie would not only make it through college, but that he would have an outstanding collegiate career.

When I arrived home, I saw a classy looking Ford V-8 convertible parked in the street behind our house. Inside, I was pleasantly surprised to be greeted by my brother Bill, who was supposed to be in Tennessee. Mother and Dad were smiling happily.

"What are you doing here, you big lug?" I said.

"I read in a Knoxville paper about my heroic little brother, and thought I better come down to see that his head didn't swell too much."

"Don't tell me that the convertible parked out in back is yours."

"Well, it just does happen to be mine, and the bank's. I completed my training, got assigned as assistant sales representative for all of Virginia, and am moving to Richmond. I got a raise in salary and bought the car from Brad when I stopped in Marietta. He gave me a good price, and the bank gave me a real good loan." Brad Olmstead, Harriet's husband, was a Ford dealer.

"Bill will be here until Tuesday when he's driving back through Marietta to have his car serviced," Dad said. "You can go with him. You won't need your car there as Brad will have transportation."

"Yes, that will work out fine," I said. "Instead of taking the train, I can ride through Georgia in the snazzy convertible."

"How did things go in Gainesville?" Mother was finally able to ask after waiting patiently for the men to finish their talking. "I'm glad you came home a day early. I hope that doesn't mean you had some trouble."

"On the contrary, we accomplished so much there was no need to stay any longer. It looks like Eddie is all set, and we'll be rooming together in one of the dorms."

During dinner, I gave the family a detailed account of our visit, and when I described the sparse room we would have, I could see Mother making mental notes of what she would look for to furnish the room the way she thought it should be.

Charles Graham called to see how the two future Gators found the university. I told him we drove through Orlando, Leesburg and Ocala, and there it was. He laughed mildly at my poor attempt to be funny. Then I filled him in on our activities.

"Considering how late Eddie learned he could possibly go, he has done very well. But it appears that you all will not get much sleep with him rising early for the cafeteria job after delivering laundry until midnight," Charles said.

"I'm told that college guys don't get much sleep during the week anyway. We can catch up on the weekends. By the way, has Lil heard anything from Sally?"

"Lil showed me a letter she received. It was mostly about thanking Lil and her family for their hospitality, and sending greetings to all the friends she had made. There was a reference to you which I could not quite understand. She wrote that she was looking forward to your visit in Marietta with some apprehension. Lil seemed to be guessing at what she meant, but she didn't share it with me."

I didn't volunteer any information, but before ending the

call I told him that Bill was home for the weekend and would probably want to play golf tomorrow afternoon. Charles readily agreed when I suggested that he join us. I called Eddie to fill out the foursome and got a two o'clock tee time at Mar-Rio Golf Course.

Out in the gazebo after supper, Bill and I swapped stories of our summer experiences the rest of the evening: his in driving a van from place to place in Tennessee demonstrating the several products his company makes; and mine with a fabulous Atlanta girl who had come down for a family visit and gone back with my heart.

Trying to prepare me for the worst, Bill said, "Even though she's very young, it sounds like she had decided to marry that guy. If she was engaged, she must have accepted a proposal."

"But while we were being abducted, she told me that he never made her feel like I do."

"That's just it. She was reacting to you under most unusual circumstances. Apparently, she had sense enough to realize that, and wanted to return to her normal life before deciding how she really felt. Don't get me wrong. I hope you win, but if you don't, you'll have a memory to treasure the rest of your life. So far, nothing like that has happened to me."

I could tell that the starlit night made Bill realize how much he had missed the river in the years since he went away to Virginia. He must have been listening to gentle waves lapping on the shore when he said simply, "I hope we will always have this place."

With most of her children there, Mother was especially happy in church the next day. With the passing years, this occurrence was becoming less frequent. When I go to college, no one will be home. The birds were certainly leaving the nest.

Since the closing of Fort Capron Country Club, on whose golf course President Harding once played, we have had only Mar-Rio Golf Course with its small pro shop and nine holes for our golfing. It is a sporty lay out, starting with the first hole bordered on the right by a sizeable canal. It behooves the slicer to aim left.

Charles and Eddie had already played nine holes when Bill and I joined them on the first tee. It was a beautiful late summer day. We gave Bill the honor, and when his drive boomed out two hundred thirty-five yards, it was apparent that he had been spending his weekends on the golf courses of Tennessee. He really enjoyed the game. Only Eddie's drive came close to matching Bill's. Charles and I had been on the beach and tennis courts this summer more than on the golf course. Yet we played respectably and, with the benefit of appropriate handicaps, finished one up on Bill and Eddie on the ninth hole of the second round. We claimed our winnings by letting them buy the Cokes and hotdogs in the pro shop.

On Monday, I went by the sheriff's office to see if there had been any developments in the murder case that I should know about before I left for Marietta. Also, Sheriff Bo had asked me to try to recall everything that I could that might have some bearing on the case, no matter how remote.

There was something. After the sheriff told me that there was nothing new, I said, "Sheriff, about midnight on the Saturday before the murder, some of us were on the Fort Capron Hotel dock after the dance. I remember seeing a cabin cruiser heading north in the river turn into Monroe Creek. It seemed to be riding a little low in the water. I thought nothing of it at the time, but lately I have been wondering about it."

"Well, the boatyard is on the creek, as well as your Dad's

place and Hoyt's ice plant," the sheriff replied. "It might have been a boat that had been taking on water and was going to Brackett's for repair. Also, there are fishing boats berthed up there."

"I know, but the only fishing boats that would be out at that time of night would be coming from the north where the ocean inlet is. However, you're probably right; there could have been any one of a number of reasons why the boat turned into Monroe Creek. It probably was going to the boatyard."

"That is the kinda stuff I want you come up with. I'll check into it, and try to find out who might have been going in the creek that night and why. Tom Brackett ought to know if it was anyone coming in for repairs."

Sheriff Bo informed me that he had taken care of the reporter from the Miami Herald. "That lady was mighty disappointed; she sure wanted that interview. She told me on the telephone that she could smell a love angle between you and that pretty Atlanta girl all the way from Miami."

I thanked Bo for his help, and told him I would contact him when I returned from Georgia.

Before returning home to pack, I went by the lumberyard and visited with Harcord, who seemed to be settling into his duties very well, although he did mention that some of the yard help resented Dad's assignment of him to work in the paint store part of the time. Harcord had heard one of them refer to him as the "boss's pet" because he had saved his little boy.

Mother did most of the packing for my trip to Marietta. While I was there, she wanted me to go shopping in Atlanta to buy some clothes for college. I assured her that I would welcome the opportunity to go to Atlanta if things turned out the way I hoped they would.

"Scott, Sally is engaged to be married. You mustn't count on seeing her when you go to Harriet's. Three magical weeks in Florida may have turned her head somewhat, but back home, very likely reality set in and she'll go through with her wedding. I just don't want you to get your hopes up, and then be disappointed. You are only just out of high school. There's plenty of time left for you to find the girl who will be your mate forever."

"But, Mother I can't imagine ever wanting any girl other than Sally. You'll be the first to know after I find out where I stand. It has been hard for me to keep from calling her before now."

On Tuesday morning, Dad woke Bill and me at six so that we could leave early enough to drive to Marietta in one day. Mother had a big breakfast cooking on the stove, which together with the box lunch of fried chicken she had prepared would hold us until we arrived at Harriet's for supper. We loaded the car in the parking area in front of the house, and with farewells from Mother and Dad, off we went to Georgia.

Going through Vero, the first town north, the odometer on the new Ford V-8 rolled over to 1,000 miles, so my brother, Bill, wasn't concerned about holding the speed down below 50 miles per hour as recommended during break-in period. The traffic was light going up Dixie Highway, the interstate road that Carl Fisher had lobbied the legislature and Congress for during the boom to lure prospective purchasers to his lots on Miami Beach. Stopping only for fuel and at a roadside picnic area to eat our box-lunch lunch, we covered the miles rapidly. On the way, Bill remarked on my long periods of silence.

"The nearer we get to Marietta, the more scared I get," I said to Bill. "The last thing Sally said to me was to call her when we get there; that she should know what she wanted to do about her future by then. I just feel that if I lose it will be hard for me to take. If she marries that fellow, it will be just because she's always been expected to. And that's no reason to marry someone."

"Scotty, you don't know the whole story. That man she's engaged to may be a fine fellow and just right for her. Sally seems to have a good head on her, and you'll just have to wait to hear her answer."

"Yes, but if the answer is the one I don't want to hear, I can't stay in Marietta for two weeks without seeing her. I'd be miserable."

"Well, if that is her answer, and you really care for her, you should bow out gracefully, and bother her no more. You will have disrupted her life enough."

We made excellent time and arrived at Harriet and Brad's house in time for supper. With Harriet right behind her, Jane, our little three-year-old niece, whom we had not seen since Christmas, came bouncing out of the front door and into my arms.

"Hey! Who is this big girl? What happened to that little girl I used to know?" I said as Jane hugged me around the neck.

"You know who I am. Quit teasing me, and come see my dog. He's got big ears," Jane replied as a lively blue-tick hound came loping around the house.

The dog stopped, sat down, and looked at me with soulful eyes seemingly worried about this guy who was holding his favorite person. I put Jane down, rubbed the dog behind his rather large ears, and we became good friends.

While all of this was going on, Bill and Brad unloaded the car and carried our luggage into the house. Harriet took me to one side.

"Sally called this afternoon asking me to tell you not to phone her tonight. She'll meet you at noon at the luncheonette in the Chattahoochee River Park. If you can't make it, I'm to let her know."

"Why can't I call her?" I asked.

"She wants to tell you in person, not on the telephone."

"I don't know if that sounds good, or sounds bad."

"I can't help you there. She didn't say anything that would indicate what her plans are." Before leaving home, I had called Harriet to tell her of the situation with Sally.

"Well, I will certainly meet her as she suggests. But how will I get there?"

"We could let you have a car, but that's not necessary. The trolley line between here and downtown Atlanta makes a stop at the park. Bill will be leaving for Virginia tomorrow morning. You can see him off, take the eleven o'clock trolley, and get there in plenty of time to meet Sally. Now let's go in. Supper is ready to put on the table."

Somehow I managed to get through the evening. Harriet wanted to know anything I could tell her about her friends in Fort Capron. When the automobile business deteriorated in Florida, Harriet had moved with Brad to the area where he was born, and it was plain to see that she missed her family and friends. Of course, I had to tell Harriet and Brad all the details of our involvement in the bootlegging murder at Manatee Creek.

Brad reminded us that during the brief period when he and Harriet lived in Fort Lauderdale, a rum-runner by the name of Alderman was executed by hanging on August 17, 1929 for murdering at sea three of the crew of Coast Guard Patrol Boat 249. The execution was carried out in an abandoned seaplane hangar at Bahia Mar Coast Guard Base directly across the bay from their home. Alderman was tried and found guilty by a federal trial jury in Miami, and Bahia Mar was the nearest federal installation, where by law the execution had to take place.

It had been a long day for Bill and me, so we retired soon after Harriet had finally convinced Jane that it was past her bedtime. Brad and Bill had decided that the mileage on Bill's new car was not sufficient to warrant a servicing, so Bill planned to leave early the next morning for Richmond, where his new home and office would be.

Everybody was up for breakfast to give Bill a good send-off. Bill wished me luck in my situation with Sally and my new school year at Florida. He recalled the times in college when toward the end of the month, the money ran out just when a big event was coming up. He told me to call on him for an extra buck or two if such an occasion rose for me, provided that situation did not happen too often. I thanked him for his good wishes and his kind offer.

Driving off in his shiny new car, Bill was the epitome of a young man thumbing his nose at the Great Depression, destined to be one of the new generation that rode the wave of better times for our country.

CHAPTER 14

The Cobb County Courthouse Square with its elegant old domed edifice and magnificent magnolias marked the end of the interurban electric railway line from Atlanta. I had been nervously waiting on a bench in the vine-covered terminal shelter when the eleven o'clock streetcar arrived on schedule. After the incoming passengers disembarked, the conductor stepped down from the car, reversed the overhead trolleys, and entered what had been the rear of the car. It now was the front.

I boarded with the other Marietta passengers, some of whom were colored folks that filed to the opposite end of the car after buying a ticket from the conductor. It was somewhat ironic that where they now sat, in the back of the car, a few minutes earlier was the front, and they would have been forbidden to sit there. I bought a ticket to Chattahoochee River Park, and found a seat off by myself, where I could watch the passing countryside and plan what I might say to Sally when we met, and after she told me her decision.

The streetcar line ran adjacent to the highway to Atlanta, going through Smyrna on the way. On either side of the eight miles to Smyrna, we passed planted fields, some of which are white with maturing cotton and others strewn with ripe watermelons. Occasional stops were made to deposit and pick up passengers at crossroads. At Smyrna, a cotton gin with waiting trucks lined up outside, was running to full capacity, and a produce market was humming with agricultural products coming and going. Beyond Smyrna, houses and stores were more frequent and fewer farms were seen.

Of course, Sally was constantly on my mind. It didn't seem possible that it was only five weeks before that I first met her that day on the beach. So much had happened since then. My mind was filled with memories: sharing the joy of Mrs. Russell's lucky night, dancing in the Terrace Room, our first kiss in the moonlit ocean, witnessing the bootlegging, the anchor-search, the abduction, escape and rescue, the awareness of love, and the parting. With the meeting so imminent, my heart pounded and I could hardly breathe.

The conductor announced our arrival at the park as we crossed over into Fulton County on the southerly side of the Chattahoochee River. Stepping off the streetcar, I went directly through the gates to the park office where I was given a map showing the location of the luncheonette. Not knowing if Sally had arrived, I thought it best to go there immediately.

A short trail through peach trees led to a large log cabin with a long porch extending its full width. Inside was a receptionist's desk in a short hall leading to the expansive eating area with its vaulted ceiling and paneled walls. A hostess was showing diners to their tables. Several tables were occupied by early arrivals being served by attractive waitresses wearing gingham aprons. I looked around and saw no sign of Sally. In response to my inquiry and description, the hostess smiled and said she had not seen her. I made myself comfortable in one of the rustic chairs on the porch, where I had a good view of the trail, and waited for Sally. It was not yet quite noon.

Several people came along the trail, but none of them was Sally. Fifteen minutes passed and I began to get anxious. In a little while, I went back to the desk to ask the busy hostess if there had been any message for me. There had been none, so I went back to the porch, uncertain as to what I should do.

It began to dawn on me that Sally might not be coming. Why would a girl like Sally, who was planning soon to marry someone she had known all her life, seriously consider breaking her engagement because she had a short summer romance with a kid just out of high school? She had arranged this luncheon meeting because she felt sorry for me, and wanted to let me down easy. At one o'clock, I knew Sally wasn't coming. Apparently, she just couldn't tell me in person, and was going to write a letter or something.

I finally left the porch of the luncheonette, and was walking despondently along the trail toward the park entrance when I heard someone behind me yell, "Scott!"

Stopping in my tracks, I closed my eyes, said an instant prayer of thanksgiving, turned around, and there was Sally running toward me. She ran into my open arms, nearly knocking me down. When we untangled, Sally said, "Where were you? I've been waiting since noon. I was about to give up."

"I have been at the luncheonette since noon waiting for you."

"The luncheonette! Oh, my gosh, I know what must have happened. I told your sister that I would meet you in the park at the launching ramp. I must have dropped a 'g'. Harriet misunderstood me and told you to meet me at the luncheonette. I have a picnic basket and a rental canoe at the launching ramp. I could think of no better way to tell you I am not getting married, as my engagement is off. It's not a sailboat—a canoe on the Chattahoochee River is the best I can do. I was going to the office to see if there was a message for me, and there you were."

"Sally, I have just endured the most miserable hour of my life, coming to the conclusion that you would go on with your life as it was before you went to Florida. I had given up. Did you really break your engagement for me?"

By then, having found a park bench, we sat holding hands, and Sally laughingly said, "Well, not entirely. The way I missed you had a lot to do with my decision, but there are other reasons. John was in Chicago at a shoe buyer's show when I came home, and not scheduled to return until Thursday. He manages his father's shoe store in downtown Atlanta. On Tuesday, I received a call from the tennis coach at Rollins College with an offer of a four-year tennis scholarship. You will remember that the day I left, I had dinner with your family, and Mrs. Konreid was there. Apparently, I have her to thank for the scholarship. The coach agreed to give me the rest of the week to consider the offer. Everything was happening so fast, I needed time to think. It was good that John was away. He's a very fine person, and my commitment to him was extremely important."

"How did you break the news to him?" I asked.

"I joined John's father in meeting him at the train Thursday afternoon. This was the first time we had been together since before I left for Florida. I had telephone conversations with John a few times while I was down there, and one time he casually remarked that I didn't seem to be at Lil's very much, especially at night. He had read the Associated Press account of our adventure in which you and I were represented as more than just friends. John's greeting to me wasn't as warm as it would have been a few weeks earlier. Anyway, before we parted we made a date to have dinner at the Elks Club that night. I devoted the rest of the day to making a final decision as to what I would do. Seeing John that brief time at the station helped. I was glad to see him, but I wasn't excited about seeing him.

"John called for me at home at six, and we drove to the club. Before going in to the dining room, I suggested that we sit out on the terrace a little while to enjoy the soft summer evening. I wanted to talk. We were supposed to marry in December, you know.

"After listening patiently to his account of the trip to Chicago and the new line of shoes that would be coming out this fall, I finally interrupted John and told him that I had been offered a scholarship at Rollins College, and that I wanted to accept it."

"That must been a shock for the poor guy. What was his reaction?" I asked.

"Well, it was a shock. At first, he said nothing, just turned his face away. Then, he reminded me that we had been planning to get married since we were youngsters living in the same neighborhood. He didn't realize it, but that was the problem. Through the years we'd let ourselves believe that it was inevitable. I agreed to the December wedding date even though I didn't feel ready for marriage. Because of this horrible Depression, I had no chance to go to college, so marrying John seemed the logical thing to do. But I now had an opportunity to go to college, and I told him that was what I wanted.

"Eventually, you came into the conversation. That was difficult to discuss. If John postponed our marriage so I could go to college, that would be looked upon as something noble. But if he gave it up because a loveable, adventuresome guy from Florida brought excitement into my life, that would be humiliating. I tried to tell him that you weren't much of a factor in my decision, but I don't think he believed me. On the terrace that night, the wedding was called off. We went into the dining room, ate a rather solemn dinner, and went to his home and told his folks. He took me home and I broke the news to my mother. She was not surprised. On Friday, I told the Rollins coach of my decision."

I stopped any further conversation by kissing her right there with people walking by. When they looked our way, I turned and said loudly so all could hear me, "You are looking at a happy man! She was going to get married. But, now she's not—she's gonna be my girl." There were some smiles and some applause even.

"Folks, don't mind him—he's just had a little too much sun. But he is kinda cute," Sally said, blushing and kissing me on the cheek. We rose from the bench and went to the launching ramp, not the luncheonette.

At the launching ramp, we checked out a canoe, loaded the picnic supplies, and embarked on the river.

The Chattahoochee River winds through the park with large trees overhanging the water from its banks. I can scull a sailboat with the rudder, or one oar, but I had to admit that I was not adept at paddling a canoe. Looking ahead in the canoe searching for a likely picnic site, Sally was happily giving directions. In a little while, she spotted a clearing and, as captain of the ship, commanded me to land there, which I did.

Ashore, kneeling in the shade of a huge live oak tree, she took from her large picnic basket a checked tablecloth, some utensils, a thermos of lemonade, and two crockery pots, one of which contained a salad of fresh Georgia peaches and apples, and the other fried chicken and biscuits.

"Now that's what I call a real feast," I said, as she spread the tablecloth on the ground and set up the picnic. "Let me at it. I haven't eaten since an early breakfast. Did you fix all this yourself? You didn't need to do that."

"As a matter of fact, I didn't. My mother prepared most of it. She and I have done a lot of talking and although she had kept it to herself, I now learn that she was less than enthusiastic about the marriage. She had wanted me to experience a part of life that she had missed. She and my father were married when she was nineteen.

"Mother seemed pleased, but a little envious, when I related the details of the exciting Manatee Creek adventure, and the times we spent together in Fort Capron. I learned that the suggestion to Aunt Mamie that I come home was engineered by John. She had no hesitancy about letting me stay the extra week. John's a shoe salesman, and Mother never saw much romance in brogans. She's glad that I have a new boyfriend, and when I told her that I was planning to meet you with a picnic in the park, she said that we must welcome this young man properly. She fried the chicken and baked the biscuits and I made the fruit salad."

"I know I'm going to like your mother, and no matter who made what, this is mighty good," I said as we devoured the crisp chicken and featherweight biscuits. We ate the fruit salad for dessert.

We cleaned up our mess, putting everything in the basket so as to leave no litter. Sally sat with her back against the trunk of the old oak tree and directed me to stretch out with my head in her lap so she could talk to me.

"You, my friend, are responsible for a big change in my life. As much as I like you and everything about you, the principal emotion I feel is freedom. It may be love later, but right now it's freedom. I now realize how organized my life was with John. I knew a month in advance what we would be doing on any particular day or night, and I accepted the fact that I was expected to be there and do whatever it was that we were to do. This included things like Elks Club socials, listening to Amos and Andy on the radio, a musicale at his sister's house, or attending a motivational seminar. The sailing I did was with my folks and their sailing club friends. John doesn't sail because his skin is sensitive to the sun. But he is a good man, and it would have been a comfortable life.

"I feel as though a burden has been lifted. I know I have obligations, but I also have new opportunities. I look forward to being your girlfriend, if you want me to be, but for now, that's as far as it goes. You can be sure that if I'm with you it is not because I feel obligated due to some relationship. No, it will be because I want to be with you. If I don't, I'll tell you."

"Sally, honey," I said, looking up into her smiling eyes, "that suits me just fine. What more could I hope for? My anxiety since you got on that train has been considerable. You feel free. I'm experiencing relief which also is freedom, freedom from anxiety. Your conditions provide us with the liberty of enjoying each other's company without analyzing all the time why we are doing what we do, or feeling what we feel."

Sally stared out across the water and absent-mindedly rubbed her hands through my hair.

"I am so glad that we understand each other. I cried all the way to Vero when that train pulled out of the station. Your friends and your folks in Fort Capron were so kind to me. I cherished the times we were together, the scary times as well the good times. I missed you so much and dreaded returning to Atlanta to face what I had ahead of me. Until the call came from Rollins, I saw no way to change things. It was then that I saw a distant light guiding me in the way I should go. I had an alternative."

I looked up at her and added, "Mother said that Mrs. Konreid was on the Board at Rollins, but it never occurred to us that she was looking you over for a tennis scholarship, logical as that appears now. Rollins has an excellent program in the minor sports of tennis and golf. The big universities hesitate to schedule tennis matches with Rollins because they often lose. What does the scholarship include?"

"Everything. I receive my room, meals and—best of all—a fine education, just the same as the other students who pay the full tuition."

"That's great, and richly deserved, but they are lucky to have you in their school. And I am double lucky to have you back in my life as my girlfriend, and going to college only a couple of hours away."

Sally pushed me out of her lap, stood up, and said, "That's enough talk about me; I haven't given you a chance to say what you did after I left. Let's go for a walk."

Hand in hand we wandered through stands of oak and maple trees, the leaves of which were beginning to show a bit of yellow, red, and gold, foretelling the promise of a brilliant autumn.

"Eddie has agreed to accept some of the money that his mother won," I said, "and is going to the university. In fact, we'll be roommates."

"Oh, wonderful! You must have noticed that I shared with him the pain of being left behind. It was no one's fault, it's just the way things were after the library board had to reduce my dad's salary when support funds were lost due to bank closings. I'm so happy for Eddie, and I suspect that you had a lot to do with it."

"Not really. He did most of it on his own," I said, and proceeded to tell Sally of the events of the previous weekend, including Eddie's need for a car to do his night-time job.

"And the answer to his need for wheels is right here in Georgia. My brother-in-law has a 1923 Model-T sedan in the lot behind his dealership that Eddie can have, as is, for fifty dollars. From what I hear it needs a little work and a few parts, but we should be able to handle that. Tonight, I'll call Eddie and tell him of the offer. Unless he has something better, I'm sure he will go for it. I wouldn't be surprised if he hopped a bus and came up here to ready the Model-T for its maiden voyage to Florida."

"You boys are something else. This world better be ready for the likes of you, Eddie, and Charles, because when you arrive on the scene, things will start humming. You thrive on challenges that demand your best efforts, and you take such delight and satisfaction in your accomplishments."

"Well, maybe you're right. We've never been short on enthusiasm."

A low-hanging oak tree limb was occupied by a perky little squirrel looking for a handout. Anticipating such a scenario, Sally had brought along a biscuit, a piece of which she daintily placed in the held-out hands of her forest friend. The squirrel nodded his furry head in thanks, popped the morsel in his mouth, and scampered up the oak tree.

Resuming our stroll along the north side of the river, I said, "We haven't talked about our schedule for the next couple of weeks. When do you go to Winter Park?"

"Classes at Rollins start the second week in September; however, I have to be there for preseason practice the week before, just after Labor Day. When does your school start?"

"It takes three days for the freshmen at the University of Florida to get organized. We go up on the sixth, but classes don't begin until Monday, the tenth."

"I have less than two weeks to do what must be done before I leave for school," Sally observed. "I didn't know I was going until last Friday. To get ready, Mother and I have made a list of the things I'll need. Busy days are ahead."

"It will all get done," I said. "By the way, don't you think that we should be getting back?" Sally agreed that we should and we began our return to the spot where we had left the canoe and the picnic basket.

"The investigation of the bootlegging and murder must be complete. Have they set a date for Paul Cochrane's trial yet?" Sally asked as we were walking along.

"A special prosecutor has been appointed by the governor. He has been working closely with Sheriff Bogar. Sheriff Bo called me in before I left Fort Capron to tell me that Cochrane is covering up for someone else who was involved in the murder, possibly another local person. I'm supposed to be listening for a voice similar to the one we heard on the beach. I told him that recognizing a voice would be highly unlikely. Cochrane and his attorney are trying to bargain for a lesser sentence, and the so-called other person may be fictitious. I had thought that this was all over, but some loose ends need to be tied up."

"It's is unsettling to know that it's not wrapped up. I don't like you to be having more conversations with the sheriff. You have helped him all you can."

"Well, I'll be home only a few days before we leave for Gainesville, so probably my only contact with him will be to discuss an interview requested by a lady reporter from the Miami Herald. Her interest is in our relationship: she assumed that we were more than just friends. I ducked her before when I didn't know myself what was happening between us. Come to think about it, I don't know what I would tell her now. I just better keep ducking."

"Yes, that would probably be best. However, I don't mind if the world knows that we are a little bit more than just friends. Sounds kinda nice."

Arriving back at our landing spot, I slid the canoe into the river and steadied it while Sally put in the basket and climbed aboard. We shoved off for an easy return downstream through the park to the launching ramp. It was then that we noticed dark clouds gathering in the west. Paddle as I might, we were yet short of our goal when a furious summer thunderstorm rolled across the park. People on land, and in boats and canoes, frantically sought shelter.

Sally turned around and trying to be heard above the wind and thunderclaps, yelled, "Here we go again! A typical date with Scott Forrester."

The brief storm passed and before long we arrived at the ramp in bright sunshine which helped somewhat to dry our wet summer-weight clothing. After turning in the canoe, we went to the luncheonette where I introduced Sally to the hostess who had suffered with me when I was waiting for her arrival at noon.

"Thank goodness, you showed," the hostess said. "I've never seen anyone so downhearted. What happened?"

We told her of the misunderstanding, how we nearly

missed each other, and about the great reunion.

"What a wonderfully romantic story! Can I do anything for you?"

"As you can see we are wet. Sally has a trolley ride into Atlanta. Do you have any suggestions about how she might dry out a bit more?" I asked.

"I do have an electric hair-dryer. Sally can use it in the employees' bathroom. Her clothes are lightweight, and that should help some."

Sally gratefully accepted the hostess's offer. They went off together and I sat in the sun on the porch hoping to dry out myself. In a little while, they returned.

"Thanks for the use of the dryer. I won't mind riding into Atlanta like this."

I also thanked the hostess. We said our good-byes and went to the park entrance.

"Sally, I'll be glad to ride into Atlanta with you."

"That isn't necessary. Daddy is meeting me at five at the Georgia Tech stop, which is only a few blocks from where we live. You need to get to your sister's. I'm sure she's expecting you for supper."

When we arrived at the park entrance, Sally hurried aboard the waiting Atlanta-bound trolley. As it left she leaned out a window, threw me a kiss, and called, "Good-bye, boyfriend. Phone me tonight after you talk to Eddie."

CHAPTER 15

From the courthouse terminal in Marietta, I walked to Brad's Ford place. While he closed his office, I went to the back lot for a look at the car he was offering to Eddie. Weeds around the Model-T were as high as the running boards. The tires had very little tread, and were soft to my kicks. Even if we got the engine running, the car wouldn't get very far without good tires. I raised the hood to look at the engine, but couldn't tell much about it without further examination which would have to wait until the next day. Very little rust was showing on the black body. I considered the offer acceptable, even generous, and told Brad so when we rode to his home on the edge of town.

Janie, who was waiting with her blue-tick hound, ran down the front porch steps and grabbed me around the legs. When I put her up on my shoulders, she squealed and laughed while the dog jumped all over me. We went into the kitchen where Harriet was fixing supper.

"Look at me, Mommy! I'm bigger than you are," Janie said.

"My goodness! Yes, you are, but slide down carefully now, Janie, I want to hear all about Uncle Scott's day in Atlanta." I let her down and she ran to Brad who had stopped to read the evening paper in the living room.

"My day was the best. It couldn't have been any better. Sally has called off the wedding, and she's going to college in Florida." I sat in a chair at the kitchen table and told Harriet the whole story. She was nearly as thrilled as I was.

"I know that you will call Mother, but I promised to call

our sister Mary as soon as I heard anything. Sally surely made a good impression on the family down there. I'm looking forward to meeting her," Harriet said.

"You probably will have to wait until this weekend. She and her mother are scrambling to get her ready for school. She must be at Rollins a week before classes begin. We didn't even make a date for me to meet her folks. I'm to telephone her tonight after I call Mother about Sally, and Eddie Russell about the Model-T."

Brad and Janie, after washing up, joined us at the kitchen table where Harriet served supper. Janie would rather talk than eat. She told a long tale about her afternoon with a squirrel in the backyard, complaining that the squirrel would run up a tree each time she tried to be friends. I told Janie about Sally sharing her biscuit with a squirrel that afternoon.

"That was a nice thing for Sally to do," she said.

"That's enough now, Janie. If you want any of that peach ice cream your daddy churned yesterday, you must clean up that plate."

Harriet had said the magic words. Brad's peach ice cream was famous in Cobb County. He was native born, but moved to Florida after the World War, returning home at the collapse of the Florida Boom. Janie liked her Daddy's ice cream, so she stopped talking long enough to eat her supper.

After dessert, Brad took Janie in for her nightly bath while I helped Harriet clear the table and wash the dishes. I told Harriet that Eddie might want to come up next week to help me resurrect the Model-T and drive it back to Florida. She assured me that it would be good to see Eddie, whose older sister Ella was a classmate of Harriet's in high school.

I first called Mother, giving her the good news, and at eight o'clock when I was rather certain that Eddie would be home, I placed a station-to-station call to him. Station-to-station long distance telephone rates were considerably less than person-to-person rates. We needed to save all the money we could.

When Eddie answered the telephone, I said, "Well, I'm here, buddy. Bill and I made good time and a lot has happened."

Eddie whooped when I told him that Sally had called off the wedding and was going to college at Rollins. I filled in the details, and then asked, "Have you done anything about getting a car for your job?"

"I've checked around without finding anything I could begin to afford," Eddie said.

"Maybe the problem is solved. Brad has a 1923 four-door Model-T which he is offering to sell to you for fifty dollars. The body and chassis seem to be okay, but it needs some tires and I haven't tried to start the engine yet."

"A Model-T engine is the simplest engine ever built. If it's not all frozen up, and we can find the necessary parts, I can get it running. You tell Brad that I'll take it. If your sister doesn't mind, I'll come up and do whatever is necessary and we can drive it back to Florida in style. The only problem is that I've promised Mr. Stoddard I would work the rest of this week to break in the new man he's hiring."

"That'll be no problem. I plan to be here for another week, and I'll find some tires and the parts we'll need before you arrive. I suggest that you drive my car to Gainesville on Sunday, leave it there and take the bus to Marietta. That'll give us a couple of days to fix and test the Model-T; then we can drive to Gainesville, drop off your car, and go on home in mine."

"Sounds good to me. We can stop in Perry and see Nell. If she approves I'll name my car "Nelly." You don't think she'll mind, do you?"

"Not at all. She's a good sport. I rather think she'll like it."

"Then 'Nelly' it will be. I better hang up. Tell Brad and Harriet how much I appreciate their help, and give Sally a hug for me; you are a lucky stiff to have a girl like that."

"Yes. How well I know. The Grahams are probably aware of Sally's decision by now, but call Lil and Charles anyway. Bring them up to date. I'll say so long."

I called Sally's number in Atlanta. Sally's father answered the phone, which scared me a little, although it shouldn't have because after I told him who I was, he was most cordial in our brief conversation.

"Sally is upstairs with her mother. I'll tell her you are calling. It was good talking to you, Scott," Mr. Graham said.

When I asked her about the trolley trip to Atlanta, Sally said, "It was fine although I was teased a bit because of my farewell to you through the window. I'm so up in the air about everything, it must show. People are so nice. I had dried out very well by the time Daddy met me. Did you talk to Eddie?"

"I did, and things are shaping up." I told her of the plan for fixing the Model-T and our return to Florida.

"That doesn't leave us much time to show you Atlanta. Mother and I are trying to get most of my shopping done tomorrow and Friday. Mother and Daddy want to see you on Saturday if it's convenient. Daddy has a half a day off from the library and they suggest a picnic at noon then tennis in Piedmont Park. Bring your racquet and some extra clothes. Mother and I will take you and Daddy on in doubles. Later you and I will have dinner and a Saturday night in downtown Atlanta. You should come to our house first."

"I have your Spring Street address, but how do I get there? I will probably be driving one of Brad's cars."

"Turn left off Marietta Street on to North Avenue just south of Georgia Tech, then left again at Spring Street and look for the number. It's not hard to find, but a city map might help. If you can find my Uncle Andrew's house on the edge of the Everglades, you should be able to find our house in the middle of Atlanta."

"I'll be there. Now, just tell me what time."

"Eleven o'clock, Daddy finishes at the library at noon." When Sally was in Florida she had said that her father was conservator at Atlanta's Carnegie Library. He was responsible for the care, restoration, and repair of the books and documents, a position he loved.

We both agreed that we would survive until Saturday without seeing each other. Since Sally was talking on the telephone in her living room in earshot of her father, our goodnights were not as affectionate as they might otherwise have been.

Thursday morning I looked over the Model-T, especially noting the self-starter which some 1923 models had, but the battery and the carburetor were missing. As far as I knew, everything else appeared to be where it should be, but the engine and transmission would need servicing with fresh oil, grease, and gasoline. This was a job for Eddie after he arrived. I would devote my time to gathering what was needed.

Brad had no tires in stock for the old Model-T, but he said his Uncle Roy ran a general store in Powder Springs, and he might have the right tires and inner tubes in the back of his store left over from earlier days. He said that Uncle Roy never ran any sales. If he couldn't sell an item in his inventory for a price that would bring him a profit, he would just keep it until someone would come along who needed that item and would pay the right price.

My sister Harriet came by and took me to the general store in Powder Springs. This gave her a chance to have me meet some of Brad's kinfolks and see the place where Brad was born. Janie was with her. She loved to visit the store because Roy's wife, Bessie, always had a treat for her.

We drove out Powder Springs Street passing the confederate cemetery, where on the slope of a hill about a half mile from the public square are graves of more than three thousand confederate soldiers marked with marble slabs. Harriet said that on April 26, Confederate Memorial Day, exercises are held there honoring those who lost their lives for the South, and not far away, at the Marietta National Military Cemetery where over 10,000 union soldiers are buried, on May 30, Decoration Day, similar exercises are held for those who gave their lives for the North. The area was the scene of some of the bloodiest fighting of the Civil War, which culminated in the Battle of Kennesaw Mountain.

Continuing on, Powder Springs Street became Powder Springs Road, and eventually we came to a junction presided over by Uncle Roy's store in a big wooden frame building with a broad roof overhanging the entrance. Uncle Roy was pumping gasoline up into a glass tank on top of the Standard Oil gas pump standing out front. When the glass tank filled, Uncle Roy pulled a lever, and the gasoline flowed through a hose into a Dodge he was servicing. Uncle Roy took payment from his customer and saw us getting out of Harriet's Ford.

"Hello, Harriet, and little Janie. If you're not a sight for sore eyes. And who might this young man be?" Uncle Roy said.

"This is my brother, Scott, from Florida, Uncle Roy. He's going to be visiting us for a few days, and we want him to meet Brad's family. Also he's looking for some car parts you might have."

"Come on in. Stay and have a bite with us. Bessie always has some lemonade in the icebox, and she'll make up some sandwiches." We, of course, agreed and followed him into the store.

Men in white aprons standing behind a long counter were waiting on customers. The interior was much like any other country store with its barrels, boxes, and shelves of canned and packaged groceries, and stacks of men's clothes and racks of ladies' dresses. I was introduced to Aunt Bessie sitting on a high stool at a cash register, taking money from cash customers, or slips from the many neighbors who had running charge accounts.

"Harriet, Janie, and Scott are going to stay and eat with us. I'll take over here while you go in the kitchen and make the sandwiches. Be sure to use that sourdough bread you baked this morning."

Uncle Roy took Aunt Bessie's place at the cash register. I stayed with him while Harriet and Jane went with Aunt Bessie to the kitchen.

"Uncle Roy, you don't happen to have some tires and tubes for a 1923 Model-T Ford, do you?" I asked.

"Let's see, maybe I do. They's a lot of different kind of tires in the back room—all new. I don't keep no used tires. If I got them they should be in good shape."

I told him why I was looking for some tires. He called over one of his clerks who wasn't busy at the moment. "Jim, this is Scott. He needs some 1923 Model-T tires. Take him in the back room and see what you can find."

Jim led the way through a door to a large storage room neatly arranged with hundreds of items of merchandise. A couple of dozen tires were in an overhead rack. Jim set a ladder up against the rack.

"Even though Model-T tires in the early twenties were almost all alike, there were some differences. It would help if I knew the size," Jim said.

"The number on the old tires was 30 x 3½," I said.

Jim moved the ladder several times looking for a 30 x 3½. I was beginning to feel discouraged when he said, "Here they are. There's a set of four, but no fifth one for a spare."

"That's great. We don't need a fifth tire. We can use the

best of the old ones for a spare."

Jim handed the tires down to me, then came down off the ladder and set the tires to one side. He went over to another shelf with a large inventory of inner tubes where he had no trouble finding inner tubes that would fit. We returned to Uncle Roy at the cash register and told him what we found, and I asked him how much I owed him.

From several books on the shelf behind him, Uncle Roy took a book marked 1923. Using an index, he found the invoice price he paid for these tires ten years ago.

"I'll give you those tires for what I paid for them, plus twenty percent. I'd like to give them to you for less, but I got to get somethin' for storin' them all these years. The total for the tires and tubes comes to twenty-four dollars."

The price was very reasonable, and probably a lot less for these hard-to-find items than I would have to pay if I located them elsewhere.

"That is more than fair," I said, reaching for my billfold.

"Oh, don't pay me now. That can wait until I deliver them to you at Brad's place tomorrow. I got to go there anyway."

We shook hands; that seemed important to the old gentleman. I thanked him and went into the kitchen for my sandwich and lemonade and found that the sourdough bread tasted much like the Bahamian bread that Harcord's mother makes.

After a visit with Aunt Bessie, we told Uncle Roy that we would look for him tomorrow and left the store to see the home where Brad was born and raised. The old farmhouse was still standing but no longer belonged to anyone in the family. It had been sold about the time that Brad left for the University of Georgia with a football scholarship.

Brad remained fiercely loyal to Georgia even after moving to Florida, where he became prosperous selling Lincoln and Ford automobiles in Vero and Fort Lauderdale. He was in Vero when he met and married my sister, Harriet. The Florida economic wonderland turned to reality, and he and Harriet moved to Georgia. The rivalry between the Bulldogs and Gators was continuous but friendly in our family.

Upon returning to Marietta, I reported to Brad my success in finding the tires at Uncle Roy's in Powder Springs. He said that a new carburetor would cost twenty-eight dollars, but that I might get one for much less at a junkyard.

That night I called Eddie again telling him of the progress I had made. He said that I need not go looking through junkyards for a carburetor because he could get one through contacts he had at the service station and would bring one with him when he came. Eddie added that his bus was scheduled to arrive at 2:10 on Monday.

Harriet was glad to hear that there was nothing more that I could do about the car and was not seeing Sally until Saturday because she had made some plans for me for Friday.

CHAPTER 16

Harriet's plans for me on Friday involved a YMCA-sponsored swimming meet. Sam Ward, one of Brad's many nephews, at Harriet's suggestion, asked me to swim with him as a member of a four-man team entered in the meet. Because I was from Florida, Sam took some razzing for running in a ringer. The officials ruled that I was eligible, and we had little difficulty winning the championship. The many events in which I was entered kept me in the pool for most of the day. I won a number of ribbons, but that wasn't all I got.

The concrete swimming pool was filled by unfiltered ground-water flowing in through a pipe at the shallow end. Chlorine was added to the water to meet Georgia Health Department standards. There being no facilities for changing clothes at the pool, I was still wearing my white bathing trunks when Sam took me to Harriet's after the meet ended.

As usual, Janie and her dog came running out to meet us. Janie stopped and said, "You look funny."

"What do you mean I look funny?" I said.

"You have green hair. I never saw anybody with green hair." she giggled.

About that time Harriet came outside. "Scotty, what happened to your hair? It's green, and so are your white trunks."

"That occurs when too much chlorine is added to the water," Sam said. "Not many guys around here have hair as blond as his or wear white swimming trunks."

Now that I noticed, I did see that my trunks were green. We went inside where I looked at myself in a mirror in the hall.

"My gosh! My hair is green! The green will wash out, won't it?"

"Yes, eventually, but not right away. If you stay in the sun a lot, I would give it about a week," Sam said.

"A week!" I exclaimed. "I'm meeting my girl's folks tomorrow. I can't show up with green hair!"

"Unless you want to shave it all off, I reckon you're going to have to. I've gotta go now. Thank you for being the star of the day, but it's too bad that newspapers don't print pictures in color. Your green hair might look pretty in the Journal tomorrow."

I told Sam that, other than the green hair, I enjoyed the day. He left for home, and I dashed for the shower.

At precisely eleven the next morning, I arrived at the Grahams' house wearing a Georgia Bulldog cap I borrowed from Brad. Sally must have heard me drive up because she came out on the porch to greet me, stopping short when she saw what I was wearing.

"What are you doing in that cap?" Sally said. "I never thought that I would see a Gator wearing a Bulldog cap."

"It's the only cap I could find, and you would have suffered a worse shock when you saw me without it," I said, hanging back until I could explain.

"Well, take it off. I want to see."

I slowly removed my cap. Sally looked at my hair and after trying to repress a snicker, she laughed out loud.

"It's not funny," I said, putting my cap back on. "I've got to meet your mother. What an impression I'm going to make!"

"You'll have to convince her that your hair is not normally green. I don't believe I have mentioned your hair. It wasn't important to me."

Dressed in a sky-blue blouse and a white tennis skirt, Sally's mother, Julia Graham, joined us on the porch. Sally's introduction was simple, "This is Scott, Mother."

I had to take my cap off. With a flicker of a startled look on her face, she graciously said, "How do you do, Scott. It's a pleasure to meet you."

"It's a pleasure to meet you also, Mrs. Graham, and I am sorry about my hair."

"Mother, I didn't want to tell you, but Scott has green hair," Sally said, sounding sincere.

To my dismay, I thought Sally's mother believed her until I saw a twinkle in Mrs. Graham's eye. "Don't worry, Scott, I know when she is teasing. Her description of you did not include green hair. Come in and tell me about it while we gather up our things. Frank said he could leave a little early and will meet us at the picnic area by the tennis courts at 11:30."

Sally and her mother led me into their comfortable home tastefully decorated in a traditional Southern style. We loaded the food, drinks, and tennis rackets into the car as I briefly related the events leading up to my acquisition of green hair. Mrs. Graham said that she had heard of others suffering the same fate.

Piedmont Park, Atlanta's largest municipal park, was but a short distance from the Graham home. One of the many tree-shaded picnic pavilions in the 185-acre park adjoined the tennis courts where Sally had learned to become a championship player. This being her first visit to the park since returning from Florida, she received a hero's welcome from the staff when we entered the tennis pro shop. They were really excited when she introduced me as the one who got her in and out of all the trouble that they had read about in the paper. Mrs. Graham had to explain my green hair. She was obviously well-known and admired, as was her husband, Frank.

Tennis is a popular sport in Atlanta. I learned that in addition to the twenty courts at this complex, dozens more were in other municipal parks, as well as at private clubs and homes. Atlanta's best known professional tennis player was Bryan "Bitsy" Grant, who had won the United States Clay Court Championship in 1930. Staff members told me that Sally had literally grown up on these courts, and they were proud of her as the high school girls' champion.

Upon Mr. Graham's arrival, introductions were made and he said, "Scott, since you and I are going to be playing together, it won't make me feel quite so old if you will call me Frank, and Sally's mother will respond to Julia, I'm sure."

"Yes sir, I'll call you Frank since you are my partner, but calling Sally's mother Julia would be hard to do even though she looks as though she should be Sally's sister."

"You're a smart young man. I'll tell her you said that. She might go easy on you at the net."

We adjourned to the pavilion, found an empty table, and enjoyed a leisurely picnic, followed by a brief rest under the nearby shade trees. Energetic Sally could wait no longer and ended our respite.

"On your feet, Scott! You made me keep going down in that jungle when all I wanted to do was sleep," Sally said, nudging me out of a siesta. Mother and I are ready to take you and Daddy on."

"Okay, okay, I'm getting up, but you interrupted a good dream. And I won't tell you who she was," I teased.

"Hey! After all I've done, you're not supposed to dream about any girl but me," Sally said.

By then, we were all awake and ready to play. At the request of the staff, we took our places on the court closest to the pro shop so they could watch the match. Volleying to warm up, it was apparent that I was in for some serious tennis. Sally spun her racquet and Frank called "smooth," which it was, and we won the serve. I asked Frank to do the honors, and the match began.

Two hours later, I ducked at the net as Sally drove a return of her father's serve by my ear, winning the second set, 7-5, after we had split the first two sets, 6-4. Applause went up from the staff and passersby who had gathered to watch what they said was an exciting match of excellent tennis.

Exhilarated but exhausted, we returned to the Grahams' house, the ladies lording it over us because of their victory. It was easy to see where Sally's talent came from. Her mother was better than any woman other than Sally that I have ever seen play. My game was as good as it gets, but it was Frank who kept us in the match.

Frank had made dinner reservations at Venable's on Forsythe Street for Sally and me. He and Mrs. Graham stayed home, leaving the evening to us. At eight, we were seated at a candle-lit table overlooking a garden in this fine restaurant. Across from me, Sally's beautiful eyes reflected the soft candlelight, her lovely face serenely relaxed in the happiness of the moment. My enchantment must have been apparent; she reached across the table, and touching my hand, said, "Your presence brings me much pleasure."

The spell was broken with the arrival of our waiter. An excellent dinner was served while a string quartet played Mozart sonatas and Strauss waltzes in the background. From the restaurant it was only a short walk to the Ansley Hotel, where Isham Jones and his orchestra were playing on The Rainbow Roof. The dinner floor show had just ended and we found a vacated table next to the dance floor and not too close to the band.

Being in love as I was, I couldn't have found better music to listen and dance to than the rich ensemble sound of Isham Jones' orchestra. At a time when many of the big bands were using bubbles, accordion runs, and extended trombone slides, the Isham Jones band was pure romance. We danced to many of the songs Isham Jones had written, including "It Had to Be You" and "I'll See You in My Dreams." When the band played our request for "Under a Blanket of Blue" it took us back to the Terrace Room of the Fort Capron Hotel. We danced every number right through to Hoagy Carmichael's "Stardust," followed by the band's theme song, "You're Just a Dream Come True." We joined other couples thanking Isham Jones and members of the band for a lovely evening. Sally got his autograph.

Downtown Atlanta was pleasantly hushed at the midnight hour when we strolled hand in hand to the car parked near the restaurant. On our way home, Sally snuggled up against me listening to Guy Lombardo's orchestra playing on the car radio. The fragrance of magnolia blossoms permeated the early morning air as we sat holding each other in the front porch swing. Between lingering kisses, Sally told me that try as she might, she could not keep from falling in love. It was a day to remember. In time, I reluctantly left her at the door and returned to Marietta.

CHAPTER 17

St. James Episcopal Church, Brad and Harriet's parish, pre-dates the Civil War. Harriet took Janie to Sunday School earlier, and Brad and I joined them for the eleven o'clock service. Most of Brad's family are Methodist and Baptist so we did not see any of them at St. James, but we went to the Wards' for Sunday dinner featuring fried chicken and Brad's famous peach ice cream.

Normally, we would have gone for a Sunday drive but Frank and Julia Graham were coming with Sally from Atlanta to meet Brad, Harriet, and Janie. They arrived late in the afternoon in time for a light supper. Harriet was delighted with Sally. Right away, they were like sisters, retiring to a bedroom to share secrets about me, I guessed. Brad and Frank found that they had common acquaintances and spent most of their time talking about the upcoming college football season. Janie was taken by Julia Graham, most likely because she patiently listened to Janie talk about her world with its dolls, squirrels, and her dog. I sat back enjoying the bonding that was apparent among these people.

Coming out of the bedroom, Harriet said, "If it's all right with you, Julia, we would like Sally to come up on Tuesday and spend the night. I know that the boys would like her help with the Model-T."

Julia said, "Sally and I are well along with college preparations and we can spare her for a couple of days."

"That way," I said, "she can be here Wednesday for the road- test drives."

It was decided that Sally would take a morning trolley to Marietta. The Grahams left for home and there was nothing more to do until Eddie arrived.

I met Eddie at the bus station when he arrived on Monday. While we were driving to Harriet's, I asked, "How was the trip, and where did you leave my car?"

"The trip was fine and your car is at Piggy Park," he replied. "Getting an early start, Charles and I were in Gainesville before noon. Maude and Annie were on duty when we stopped to eat. They remembered me, and after I told her of our plan, Maude suggested that I leave the car in a shed at the back of the parking lot. I readily accepted and after finishing our meal, I drove around the campus to show Charles our dormitory and other points of interest. We returned to Piggy Park, put the car in the shed, and got out on the highway to hitchhike to Jacksonville."

"Did you have any trouble getting a ride?"

"Not at all. A man was going to Jacksonville after having taken his son back to school from a weekend visit at home. He stopped in response to Charles's well-positioned thumb and took us right to the bus terminal. Charles caught the first bus to Charlotte, which is close to Davidson College. I ate supper and went to a nearby movie since my bus didn't leave until after midnight. So, here I am."

"From the looks of that box you had with your suitcase, I presume you have the carburetor," I said.

"I sure have and it cost me only eight dollars."

We arrived at Harriet's where Eddie put his suitcase in my room. Harriet asked Eddie about his sister, Ella.

"You must tell me all about her. It's been quite a while since we used to sip sodas at the drugstore. But I know you're anxious to get over to Brad's. We will talk about it tonight," Harriet said.

We drove to the Ford place and went in to Brad's office to complete Eddie's purchase of the Model-T.

"I've got the title right here ready to transfer to you as soon as you take a look at the Model-T and are sure you want it," Brad said.

"I don't need to see it. How could I be hurt getting a four door Model-T sedan for fifty dollars? Here's the money," Eddie said, taking two twenties and a ten out of his billfold.

Brad signed over the title, and Eddie was the proud owner of his first automobile. He made a production of walking through the service area out to the back lot. Nelly was there waiting for him.

"She looks better than I expected; the finish is good and the windshield and windows aren't even cracked," Eddie said as he inspected the Model-T he had just bought. "The first thing we gotta do is move her out of these weeds." With the help of one of Brad's mechanics we pushed Nelly to a sur-faced area.

"It hurts to see her sitting there on worn out flat tires. Let's jack her up and put the new ones on," Eddie said.

We found a jack, lug wrench, and pump under the rear seat. With a little lubrication the jack worked fine. We soon had the old tires off and the new tires on and inflated. The wooden spokes were in need of cleaning, which we did while the wheels were off. The cleaning of the interior was left for Sally.

"The radiator is liable to be stopped up after sitting here for so long," Eddie said. "Brad has probably got some sodium hydroxide powder which is a caustic we can use to make radi-ator cleaner. We mix it with water, fill the radiator, and leave it in there while I swap the carburetor. After I make the exchange, we will flush out the radiator and it should be clean. The sodium hydroxide cuts the grime without harming the metal."

Eddie had some trouble removing the old carburetor but after about an hour, the one he brought with him was installed. Using a hose from the garage we flushed the cleaner out of the radiator but left it filled with water so we could check it for leaks in the morning.

We drained the old oil from the crankcase and what little gasoline was remaining in the gas tank. The drained oil and gasoline were deposited in a drum that Brad kept for that purpose.

Brad called to remind us it was time for supper. We left, pleased with the progress that had been made. During the evening Eddie told Harriet the latest about his sister, Ella. She is a nurse at Capron General Hospital, much admired in the community for her selfless devotion to the patients. She has had little time for anything other than her work. However, a widower doctor has taken a definite interest in Ella. Harriet was pleased to hear that.

"Ella was one of my favorite friends in high school. We used to sit in the Sunrise Soda Shoppe sipping sodas watching the boys go by. They sometimes teased her about her shyness, but she didn't mind, she was a real good sport. And I never heard her say a bad word about anyone. She always looked for the good in people. After receiving her degree from the Florida College of Nursing, she devoted her life to caring for others, never thinking of herself," Harriet said to Eddie.

"I know what you mean," Eddie replied. "Although she seems very happy, I have worried that she did not have much of a social life. But now she and that doctor are going out, and she may have just been waiting for the right man to come along."

"That could be. Anyway, you can see how pleased we were that you could spend a little time with us. When you get home, be sure to tell her that I was asking about her."

Anxious to get on with our project, Eddie and I wakened early, ate some corn flakes, and were working on Nelly just as soon as Brad's garage was opened. There was no evidence of any leaks in the radiator.

The next task was to grease the joints in the car. For this Nelly must be put up on a rack. There were only two grease racks at the garage, but one was empty. Rather than trying to push the Model-T up on the rack we got the engine running and drove Nelly up. Her 6-volt battery was being charged, but wouldn't be fully charged until that afternoon. We had started the engine using the crank hanging down below the radiator.

We poured five gallons of fresh gas in the tank and put some oil in the crankcase. With the crank, I turned the engine over slowly a few times to pull the gas into the carburetor, and so Eddie could check the magnetic spark. He got into the driver's seat, turned the ignition key, pushed the spark lever up all the way, and pulled the hand throttle down about half way. Upon his signal, I cranked a full turn. The engine coughed and died.

"I forgot to choke it," Eddie said, as he pulled out the choke to give the engine more gas.

I cranked again, and the engine backfired with a loud "blam!" One of the mechanics in the garage stuck his head out the door and yelled, "You're givin' it too much spark."

Eddie lowered the spark lever a little. Once more, I pulled the crank. The engine coughed twice and caught up with a steady beat interrupted by a couple of bangs before Eddie pulled the spark lever all the way down and adjusted the throttle to an idling speed. I joined the cheer that rose from the observing mechanics. Nelly's engine was really running.

Eddie invited me into the passenger seat and we took a trip around the block before he drove Nelly up on the grease rack. I opened the door to step out, nearly forgetting that we were six feet off the ground. We descended safely, and Eddie began his preparations while I left for the bus terminal to meet Sally.

Sounding several extra clangs the trolley came in to the terminal with Sally pulling the bell cord. Unable to resist her playful charm, the motorman had let her celebrate the arrival. She bounced out the door carrying an overnight bag that got in the way when I gave her a hug and a kiss.

After dropping Sally's things off at Harriet's, we went to Brad's where one of the mechanics was pushing Nelly off of the grease rack with Eddie steering. He let the Model-T coast to a shady spot where the additional work would be done. Eddie and Sally happily greeted each other although without hugs—he hadn't had a chance to clean up since finishing the grease job.

"When you left on that train in Fort Capron, I didn't know if ever I would see you again. Certainly not this soon in your home state of Georgia," Eddie said.

"I'm just as amazed as you are," Sally replied. "The last two weeks have been like an impossible dream."

"How do you like my car?"

"It's beautiful. Nell will be so proud that you named it for her."

"Do you think so? I've been kinda scared to tell her. I'm going to have to let her know soon because we'll see her in Perry on the way to Florida. When we do, I want Nelly to look her best. That's where you come in. The inside is kinda dirty, and I could sure use your help."

"That's what I'm here for. So let's get started," Sally said, opening the rear door.

"Whew, is it dusty, and look at the cobwebs! If I'm not mistaken, some mice have been riding around in here. A whisk broom, brush, some rags soaked in Energine, and lots of elbow grease should make a difference."

"It's time to take a break. I'll go inside and wash up. We can get whatever you need during the noon hour. I'm sure Scotty'll be glad to help you this afternoon while I install the battery, replace the belts, and get the starter working."

"You actually have a self-starter?" Sally asked.

"Yes," Eddie replied. "It was an option on 1923 Model-T Fords, as was the speedometer. We'll find out if the starter works this afternoon, but it will take a road trip to test the accuracy of the speedometer."

After a Coke and hamburger for lunch, we went to Harriet's to borrow a broom and a brush. There were plenty of rags at the garage, but we went by Kress's five and dime store for the Energine.

I didn't help much because it took a woman's touch to clean the old car's interior properly. All I did was remove the seats and tools. With her dark hair wrapped in a bandanna, Sally went to work with a vengeance. Using the whisk broom and brush, she removed the dust and dirt from the floor and every crack and cranny, she washed the sliding windows and windshield, wiped the steering wheel and interior sides and ceiling, shined the dashboard, and finally cleaned the seats with the Energine. The inside of that Model-T looked and smelled like a new car.

In the meantime, Eddie had installed the charged-up battery under the floorboards, replaced the belts and now was ready to try the starter. He had me sit in the driver's seat. With a screwdriver in his hand and his head in the raised hood, he signaled me to step on the starter button. I pressed down with my heel but nothing happened. Eddie made some kind of adjustment with his screwdriver, and told me to try again. I did, and with a grinding sound the starter turned over the engine, slowly at first and then faster. He signaled me to stop.

"The starter seems to be working. Now it's time to see if it will actually start the engine," Eddie said.

He showed me where to set the throttle, spark and choke and how to adjust them when the engine started. I had driven Model-Ts plenty of times, but he wanted to be sure I did it just right.

He resumed his position under the hood. I was still in the driver's seat. I turned on the ignition, pressed the starter button, and after a few grinds, the engine started. I pushed in the choke and adjusted the spark and throttle, and Nelly was running as smoothly as a four-cylinder Model-T could.

Eddie closed the hood, stepped back, and smiled a smile of satisfied accomplishment, and said, "We've done all we can do, it's all up to Nelly now."

Our trip to road-test the car was scheduled for the next day, so after we washed the car and Brad's mechanics gave their approval of the way Nelly's engine was running, we drove around town listening for any possible transmission problems. Eddie chauffeured while Sally and I sat in the back seat feeling rather ritzy in the new-looking vehicle.

Having promised Uncle Roy that we would try to visit him and Aunt Bessie when we got the Model-T going, I told Eddie how to drive out Powder Springs Road to the general store. Uncle Roy looked the car over top to bottom while Aunt Bessie and Sally got acquainted. We all gathered inside for a glass of Aunt Bessie's lemonade. Uncle Roy put his stamp of approval on Nelly, and congratulated Eddie on his work. Aunt Bessie was obviously captivated by Sally's lively personality. We thanked them for their hospitality and returned to Marietta in time to take Janie for a ride before supper.

Nelly's lights worked properly so we went for a short drive after dark. Eddie had planned that we take a day to test the car on a trip in the vicinity, but when we got back to Harriet's he said it had run so well today that he didn't think the test tour was necessary.

"We'll be driving through Perry where Nell lives. That's one hundred thirty miles down the road. If we have any trouble with the car, we can fix it there," Eddie said.

"That makes sense to me," I said, and it occurred to me that Sally might go with us as far as Perry if she could.

When Sally, Eddie, and I discussed the change in plans, I suggested to Sally that she could just as well spend the day riding to Perry as driving around North Georgia and then take the bus back to Atlanta after spending the night with Nell. Phone calls were made to Nell and Sally's mother. My suggestion was agreeable provided we stop at the Grahams' on the way through Atlanta. The matter was settled, and we would leave after breakfast the next morning.

Before retiring, a phone call came for me. It was Sheriff Bogart. After exchanging pleasantries, I listened and let him talk.

"Scotty, we have a tip that a lot of the bootleg liquor that has been passing through Fort Capron is ending up in Atlanta. An address for some kind of establishment up there has been given us. I could call the Fulton County sheriff and ask him to check it out, but this is so sensitive I'd rather not let anybody there know we have the information. It could jeopardize the safety of our informant."

He hesitated and then continued, "I was wondering if you could ride by and let me know what kind of place it is. I don't have to know right away. You could call me or wait until you get home. Of course, you don't have to do this. But if you did, it might help put this thing to rest. When are you coming home?"

"Eddie Russell is up here now," I replied. "We're driving

home in an old Model-T and, barring any difficulties, we should be there by Friday evening."

He gave me the address and said, "If you do decide to find out what is at that location, Friday will be soon enough to let me know unless you see something that you think I might oughta know sooner. Tell your sister and Brad hello for me. We sure do miss them around these parts."

"What was that all about?" Harriet asked.

"Nothing important," I said. "Sheriff Bo just wanted to bring me up to date on the Paul Cochrane situation. I expected he might call. He said to tell you and Brad hello and that folks miss you."

In our room, I told Eddie of the nature of Sheriff Bo's phone call. "It's very strange," I said. "The address Sheriff Bo gave me is 210 Spring Street. Sally lives on Spring Street."

CHAPTER 18

Good-byes were said the next morning. Janie cried, not because her uncle was leaving, but she was going to miss the pretty lady who had been her roommate for one night. I thanked Harriet for all that she and Brad had done for us. She assured me that they would try to get home for Christmas. Janie did insist that I hug her dog before leaving, which I did.

Having filled the gasoline tank at Brad's, we were on our way to Atlanta with Eddie driving and Sally and I in the back seat as usual. At Georgia Tech, we turned left off Marietta Street and drove the short distance to Sally's house. Frank Graham was at the library, but her mother was there with plenty of instructions. We promised to be careful and gave her Nell's address and telephone number. Julia Graham called Mrs. Stone in Perry to be certain that she was in complete agreement with our plan. She said that she was, and that they were looking forward to meeting the girl they had heard so much about.

Although Sally assured me that she knew the way through Atlanta to US 41, which was the highway we would be taking south, I asked if they had a map of Atlanta for Eddie to study. Sally found one in a desk drawer and handed it to Eddie, and we took it into another room where the light was better and looked for Spring Street.

"This may be the answer to our concern. Spring Street crosses Marietta Street, goes through downtown Atlanta past the railroad terminal to Peters Street, and to Stewart Avenue which is US 41," I said tracing the route with my finger.

"Yeah," Eddie replied, "That is the best route to take. We

will look for 210 Spring Street to see what, if anything, is going on there."

We returned to the parlor where Sally and her mother were planning their activities for later in the week. Eddie announced that we would be taking the Spring Street route through downtown Atlanta.

"Well, congratulations on your decision," Sally said. "That's the route that everybody takes when going south."

We were willing to overlook Sally's sarcasm, because we had found what we were looking for, the route of Spring Street. Julia Graham had gone outside to see Nelly. She patted the hood and said, "Nelly, get them as far as Perry. The boys are on their own after that."

That we were not including Sally in on the quest caused me a feeling of some guilt, but I was afraid it might cause her some worry. At my suggestion that she show us points of interest, Sally sat in front with Eddie. This would give me an opportunity to look at the numbers without being obvious.

As we drove along, the house numbers got smaller until we reached the busy railroad terminal, which apparently was the numbering dividing line. South of the terminal, our guide said, "On your right is the Fulton County Fish Market. It's the biggest fish market in Georgia. Seafood arrives daily from both coasts of Florida." The number on the sign in front was 210. Eddie and I exchanged quizzical looks. What could a fish market have to do with anything?

Suddenly, Eddie pulled over and parked.

"What are you doing?" I asked.

"I just had an idea. According to Sally, seafood arrives daily from Florida. Nell loves Fort Capron shrimp. Let's take her some."

"Let's do," Sally said. "Packed in ice, the shrimp will be fresh when we get to Perry."

Walking back to the fish market, I began to understand what Eddie was doing. In addition to taking a nice gift to our hostess, we would have an opportunity to look around 210 Spring Street and see if any of the activity there had any connection with the Manatee Creek murder case.

The market was a very busy place at that hour of the morning. With the help of Sally, who had been there many times, we learned that the shellfish and shrimp were sold at a stand in the rear of the building. Eddie bought a two-pound box of shrimp and had the box packed in ice.

"If these shrimp are from Florida, how do I know they are fresh?" Eddie asked the clerk serving him.

"These shrimp were caught in the ocean off Fort Capron yesterday and shipped up here in a refrigerated freight car last night. They've been on ice since they were caught and headed."

Eddie thanked him for the information. I could see an unloading dock out the rear door by a railroad siding. The market was not only a retail store to buy fish, it appeared to be a distribution center also. Men were rolling barrels from the loading dock to trucks outside a side door.

Having done what Sheriff Bogart asked us to do, we continued our trip through the rest of Atlanta and out onto the highway. As we passed through Hapeville, we saw a sign indicating that Jonesboro was 10 miles down the road. There was little traffic on the highway so Eddie set our speed at 35 miles per hour. Twenty minutes later we arrived at Jonesboro; our speedometer was reasonably accurate.

At noon we arrived at Barnesville, and Sally suggested that we stop at a lunch room she knew about near the campus of Gordon Military College. Place mats on our table noted that General Lafayette had passed the night at a nearby plantation home on a return visit to the South in 1825. I was beginning to feel like we were on a tour.

So far, Nelly had been serving us well, but we still had about 60 miles to go before we got to Perry. This time, Sally joined me in the rear seat. We stopped at a garage to fill the gas tank and radiator. In the 75 miles we had come since Marietta, we had used five gallons of gasoline and a lot of water. It was a hot day.

We passed through the peach country for which Georgia was famous. Sally provided us with another tidbit: Fort Valley which we came to next was originally named Fox Valley for the many foxes in the vicinity, but when the name was sent to the post office department in Washington it was misread and recorded as Fort Valley.

The Stone home was one of the few antebellum homes still standing in Perry. We easily found the simple white frame house which was unique for the iron-railed porch with steps at both ends. Pulling up into the driveway fronting on one end of the porch, Eddie squeezed the bulb of our horn, loudly sounding our arrival.

Sally and I stood back while Eddie and Nell had their reunion, which was comparatively subdued on Eddie's part since Nell's mother was with her and meeting him for the first time. Handing Nell the box of shrimp, Eddie said, "Here, I brought you a present from Fort Capron."

"Well, from the smell, it isn't roses, so it must be shrimp. Mama, look what we have - Fort Capron shrimp! You don't get them at the Perry Piggly Wiggly."

After the introductions, it was apparent that Mrs. Stone was a lot like Nell, and she and Eddie were finding it easy to get to know one another. Sally and I were included in the greetings, and soon we were hearing of the party that Nell had hastily arranged for that evening to meet her friends.

Finally, Eddie said to Nell, "I've got someone I want you to meet." Nell had not paid much attention to our method of transportation until he took her by the hand and led her to the driveway where the Model-T was resting.

"This is Nelly," he said, and proceeded to tell Nell how he happened to have the car, and that he had officially named the car Nelly, unless she objected.

"Heck, no! If she is as great as you say she is, I'm proud to have her named after me. With that name, it will be like me being there all the time, and you're going to feel guilty if you take any of those Florida floozies for a moonlight ride."

"That's telling him, Nell," Sally said. "I'll bet that never occurred to Eddie when he named her and now he's stuck with it. We don't need to worry too much though, even if we cared, because there are no girls at that monastery they're going to."

The party that night was outside in the garden lit by Japanese lanterns and a full moon shining through century-old oaks. Throughout the evening the young people square-danced to lively bluegrass music provided by a fiddler and banjo picker. At midnight, the party broke up with a lot of "bye kows" and "y'all come backs". Happy memories of Georgia hospitality were stored away by the two Florida boys.

When Eddie and I retired to our bedroom, we discussed our visit to the fish market.

"What did you think about those barrels being rolled out the door?" I asked Eddie.

"That just appeared to be distribution of the seafood like big fish markets do," Eddie replied.

"But how do you know it was seafood in all of the barrels? I've always heard that for safer transport each bottle of bootleg booze is wrapped in straw and sewed up in burlap as "hams." A "ham" consists of 6 quarts or 12 pints. It would be easy to slip in a barrel of "hams" among the legitimate seafood. I think I better call Sheriff Bo when we get to Gainesville tomorrow."

Eddie and I got an early start the next morning. My light-hearted farewell with Sally was in sharp contrast with our last farewell. She agreed to go with me to the Stetson football game only three Saturdays away if it did not conflict with some obligation she might have at Rollins. Nell was to take her to the bus station later in the morning for the return trip to Atlanta. Eddie asked Nell to think about coming to Gainesville for Fall Frolics at the end of the football season.

The distance from Perry, Georgia to Gainesville, Florida is 225 miles. Figuring an average speed of 25 miles an hour we had nine hours of driving time ahead of us if all went well. Breezing along nicely we passed through Vienna, and made a stop at the Ford place in Tifton to get some fuel, and check the water in the radiator, which was our greatest concern. The salesmen and mechanics were interested in Nelly because 1923 was the first year that Ford made four-door Model-T sedans. The mechanics told us that Nelly's water pump and radiator were doing fine. We decided that we could pick up the speed a little. We had made only 40 miles.

I took over the driving and shortly after noon we were approaching Valdosta when I noticed Nelly was trying to pull to the right. We stopped and saw that the front right tire was going flat. Eddie examined the tire and found the nail I had run over, puncturing the tube.

We drove off of the road to the shade of a pecan tree. "This is what I've been doing all summer," he said. "I'll have it fixed in no time."

"Be my guest," I said, "I'm glad that it is you and not me. If you don't mind I'll stretch out in the shade and watch."

Eddie got the jack, lug wrench, and inner tube repair kit from under the rear seat. In no time, he had the tire off and the tube out. He located the hole and patched it and put the tube back in the tire.

"Now, it's your turn," he said, handing me the hand pump. I had no choice but to get up from my relaxing reverie and fasten the air hose to the valve and proceed to pump up the tire. His job required brains, mine needed brawn. I began to see a pattern to our way of life together.

We drove on into Valdosta which was a good-sized town used by travelers to and from Florida as a convenient stopping place. We didn't stay long as our tire trouble put us behind schedule and Gainesville was still more than one hundred miles away. We could afford no more mishaps.

At six o'clock, we walked into the Piggy Park. "Hey girls, we made it! How about something to eat?" Eddie yelled.

"Glory be," Maude exclaimed, "if it ain't those little south Florida rats. I thought a cat would have had them by now. Annie, you better make up some extra burgers."

Maude and Annie fed us well. It was between sessions and not many students were in the diner. The first thing Maude wanted to know was how things went with Sally and me. She was happy for me when she heard the story. We filled the girls in on the rest of our trip, and they told us that my car was still in the shed and that we could put Nelly in its place if we wanted. It being only seven, Eddie and I decided to take them up on their offer and drive on to Fort Capron tonight. I would call the sheriff in the morning.

I backed my car out of the shed, and Eddie drove Nelly in after showing her off to Maude and Annie. He was really proud of that Model-T and the way she had performed the last two days. Eddie called Mr. Strickland, the laundry owner, at home and assured him that he was all set with transportation.

At eight, we bid our new friends goodbye and said that we would see them next week. The drive home was uneventful; our families were happily surprised to see us a day early.

Chapter 19

Mother wanted to hear all about my visit with Harriet's family. She missed seeing them, especially Janie because she's growing up so fast. I told her of Sally's decision and my time with her folks. She was pleased that Mrs. Konreid had arranged the scholarship offer so that Sally would have the opportunity to go to college.

"It's none of my business, of course, but Sally did not seem ready for marriage. Her parents must be very nice. I would love to meet them."

"Maybe you will sometime. If things go the way I'm hoping, you will be seeing more of Sally," I said.

I telephoned Sally and learned that she had returned home without incident, except that it was a rather hot bus ride. She had only two days remaining before her parents would take her to Rollins on Labor Day. She had a busy schedule. I thanked her mother for letting Sally go to Perry with us.

Instead of calling Sheriff Bogart, I went by his office to tell him of the activity at 210 Spring Street and my theory about "hams" in the barrels.

"In the earlier days, 'hams' of bootleg whiskey were shipped north in what was supposed to be barrels of iced-down fish, but after the federal agents got wise to it, the bootleggers switched to fast automobiles with special springs," Sheriff Bo said. "Maybe they're slipping a few barrels through again. I'll have to give this some thought. We're not going to get any more information from our informant. We think he has skipped the country, or is dead."

"I can't imagine Roger Hoyt having anything to do with this," I observed.

"No. Putting the 'hams' in the barrels is always done at the fish house, not the ice plant. There is no reason to suspect him. There are plenty of fish houses up and down the coast where this could be done. I thank you and Eddie for going by 210 Spring Street. By the way, how is Sally?"

"Just fine. Bragitta Konreid arranged a tennis scholarship for her at Rollins. We had a good time in Georgia. She may be coming up for the Stetson game later this month."

"Sounds like you got something good goin' there. She's a mighty fine girl. I haven't heard anymore from the Miami Herald reporter. When are you and Eddie going to Gainesville?"

"We leave next Thursday. You ought to see the Model-T Eddie got from Brad. He named it 'Nelly' after Nell Stone. We stopped by Perry where Nell lives on the way down to Gainesville. She got a kick out of it."

After leaving the sheriff's office, I went to Eddie's house. His mother was most grateful for the progress he has made. We discussed things we would need for our dormitory room. She was in the process of making curtains for the windows; they were orange and blue, the school colors.

It was late when I had arrived last night and Dad had left for work before I got up, so we went to his office to visit with him, and tell him of our trip. We stopped in the lumber yard to see Harcord. He was doing fine; at the moment he was surrounded by a bunch of Boy Scouts decorating one of the trucks as a float for the Labor Day parade.

Scheduled as part of the Labor Day celebration were sailboat races in which Eddie and I would sail my boat. After lunch at Stoddard's, we careened Lively Lady on the rivershore in front of our house, and cleaned and waxed her bottom, and took her out in the river for a sail to check her rigging. It was a beautiful day on the water; with its slick bottom, the boat sailed especially fast. We would be hard to beat in our class.

It was not an important regatta, but very competitive with boats mostly from Fort Capron, Stuart, and Vero. We raced in different classes divided according to sail area. The main competition in our class was Tom Brackett's brothers, Buddy and George; the ice plant owner, Roger Hoyt; and a photographer, Larry Hall. One heat was to be held in the morning and two in the afternoon. There were reports of a tropical storm making up in the Caribbean, but it was predicted to go south of Cuba.

By Monday, the storm had turned toward the northwest and was going between Cuba and the Florida Keys. Fort Capron was close enough to feel the effects of the storm resulting in near gale-force winds during the races. In the first heat, when we were heading for the finish line, a strong gust hit us just as we hastily tacked over to cover our nearest competitor, Roger Hoyt. Our main sheet jammed and over we went, filling the boat with water. We got no points for that heat, but during the lunch break, we righted Lively Lady, bailed her out, and took the second place trophy by winning the two afternoon heats. Roger Hoyt finished first in the heat in which we capsized and second twice in the afternoon, taking home the first place trophy in our class.

When Eddie and I congratulated Hoyt at the awards ceremony, he said, "You boys need to watch what you're doing. When you take too many chances, you sometimes wind up all wet."

The Labor Day celebration marked the end of a very special summer for me. The time had come for completing the final preparations for the transition to life as a college student. With my car loaded inside and out with luggage and boxes,

Eddie and I left home on the following Thursday. On the way, we stopped at Rollins in Winter Park to have lunch with Sally and watch her practice with the team. Compared to ours, her dormitory room was quite plush, and the tennis facilities were the best.

We met the coach who told us that Sally had a very good chance of making the traveling team. She said that there was nothing scheduled for Saturday of the Stetson game and Sally would be permitted to go to the game with me in Gainesville provided I got her back by ten o'clock that night. Sally had a teammate from Gainesville who was going home that weekend who would give her a ride up on Saturday morning. It was no problem for me to drive her back to Rollins after the game.

In high spirits and with youthful exuberance, Eddie Russell and I rolled on up the road to our future and joined hundreds of other students in moving into rooms in the University of Florida dormitory complex. Many parents were there to add to the confusion. Seeing the embarrassment of some students whose parents were reluctant to leave their child in this new world, we were glad that our folks had enough confidence in us to let us move in on our own. The day was completed by a visit to Piggy Park, where we had supper with Maude and Annie and got Eddie's car.

Bewilderment was the name of our first two days of college life. It was as if we had never had orientation. Registration, course selection, and classroom assignments were to be completed by all students, not just freshmen. Lines were long and tempers short, but somehow it was accomplished. In addition, Eddie learned how to make doughnuts and was otherwise trained for his job at the cafeteria, which was to begin Monday morning at six.

Sunday was a quiet day until the dormitory monitor came into our room to say that there was a telephone call for me. I took it in the booth on our floor. It was Sheriff Bogart.

"Your dad didn't much like the idea, but he gave me your dormitory telephone number. I hate to bother you, but I just thought that I should keep you posted until we wrap this thing up. We don't have no further idea who from around here might have been involved, but our investigation leads us to believe that someone from Levy County was high up in Cochrane's organization. Levy County is between Gainesville and the Gulf of Mexico. It seems everywhere you go there is something or someone connected to this situation. There ain't nothin' you can do; I just wanted you to know."

I thanked the sheriff and, in answer to his questions, told him we were well settled and ready for classes to begin.

"Eddie," I said, "it looks like the sheriff and the feds are having a hard time closing out this murder case. They still think someone local is involved, but don't know who, and have some kind of lead on someone in Levy County. Maybe they're too close to the forest to see the leaves."

"What do you mean?"

"Let's you and me solve this case, so Sally and I can relax and go on with our lives."

"I'm willing, but where do we start?"

"We start by narrowing it down to the two questions to which we need to know the answers. One: who is the local man involved, and two: who is it in Levy County and what is his connection?"

"Do you have any ideas?" Eddie asked.

"I can't prove it, but everything I know seems to point to Roger Hoyt."

"Oh, man! That can't be. You said that the sheriff doesn't suspect him."

"He doesn't, but I do. The suspicious looking boat I saw on the night of the dance turned into Monroe Creek and his ice plant is on Monroe Creek. Bootleg whiskey is shipped out in barrels packed at fish houses. Although he is primarily an ice plant owner, I'll bet an investigation will reveal that he owns one or more of the fish houses. Hoyt and Cochrane both went to Stetson University and came on the political scene about the same time. And, finally, remember the remark he made at the award ceremony, about taking chances and winding up all wet? It sounded like a warning to me."

"What are you going to do about it?"

"Nothing now, because I have no proof. We just have to bide our time and see what happens. As for the guy in Levy County, we have nothing to go on. But since it is nearby, let's get in my car and take a ride just to see what's there."

We found that the Levy County road goes southwest from Gainesville through pine forests at first, and then low-lying grass and pond lands for a total of about fifty miles to the Gulf of Mexico. We went through Bronson, the county seat, but did not stop until we got to Otter Creek, where we saw a grand-motherly-looking gray-haired woman tending a vegetable garden alongside her one-story frame house with a creek running by. She appeared to be a person who could give us some information about Levy County.

We stopped and talked to the lady, who was a little cautious at first, not necessarily willing to share her business with a couple of strangers. Once she looked us over and figured we must be all right, we found her to be a kindly lady who folks referred to as Aunt Ellen. She invited us to sit a bit on her back porch overlooking the creek and have a drink of water from the pitcher-pump. Aunt Ellen had been a trained nurse in the World War and was the nearest thing to a doctor west of Bronson. She had set the bones and stitched the cuts of most of the kids in the area, and delivered many of them as babies. The only politician she knew of was their state representative in Tallahasee by the name of McCurry but she did not say much about him. He lived in Bronson.

Twenty miles further on was the Gulf and the fishing village of Cedar Key. Over a little bridge to the key was a clus-
ter of weather-beaten homes, a small store, and a fish house.
At a pier out into Waccasassa Bay, a substantial looking
houseboat, two Sportsfisherman Cruisers, and smaller boats
were moored. A mate was hosing down one of the cruisers
from which four men were disembarking.

We went into the store, but watched the men coming
down the pier and get into a Cadillac parked at the foot of the
pier. The storekeeper told us that Joe McCurry, a member of
the Florida House of Representatives, had taken some of his
Tallahassee friends out for a fishing weekend. The Cadillac
drove off, and after having a supper of fried mullet and grits
in the store's cafe, we returned to Gainesville and our dorm
knowing a lot more about Levy County than when we had left.

Sally was so much a part of all of this that I felt compelled
to share with her my suspicions, which I did when I called her
later that evening. At Rollins, she had a telephone in her dormitory room. I even told her of being on the lookout for 210
Spring Street in Atlanta. She was a little put out for having
been uninformed about that situation, but understood that I
had thought it was in her best interest. We ended our conversation on a lighter note as she told me that she would be at the
student center at eleven on Saturday morning. We were excited about attending our first football game together.

I awoke only briefly as Eddie climbed out of the lower
bunk to begin his job as a doughnut-maker on Monday morning. Later, he waved to me from the kitchen as I went through
the cafeteria line for breakfast. He was finished in time to join
me as we walked to our first classes, which were in different
rooms in a nearby building. Our courses and schedules
weren't the same.

Each of our days began in a similar fashion that first week, and at night Eddie made dry runs through the swamps getting acquainted with potential customers for the laundry pick-ups and deliveries. Rush Week was underway at the campus fraternities. Both of us received invitations to fraternity rush parties but we turned them down since we decided to defer joining a fraternity until the next semester.

I had taken advantage of the opportunity that every student had to get an extra ticket in the student section. I got one for Sally. Ever ready to earn an extra dollar, Eddie had arranged to sell hot dogs in the stadium at the game. Florida had been close to winning the Southeastern Conference championship the last few years, and though Stetson was well known for having a scrappy team, the experts predicted an easy victory for Florida.

I was at the student center early on Saturday, eagerly awaiting the arrival of Sally. Right on time, her friend drove into the carport entrance, with Sally waving out the passenger window. Her friend stayed long enough to allow me to thank her and assure her that I would be taking Sally back to Rollins before ten. Sally was dressed in a blue skirt and a light white jacket, and wearing bobby sox and saddle oxfords. Her eyes shone as I pinned on her a small orange pompon corsage tied with a blue ribbon and lightly kissed her smiling face.

After a lunch in the student center, we were walking to the stadium when I saw a car with Georgia license plates in a wooded parking area across the street. A man sitting in the car surreptitiously handed an envelope to none other than Roger Hoyt.

"Don't look now, Sally, but I think I see our mayor receiving payment for some goods for which he arranged delivery in Atlanta." Of course, she looked and saw the Georgia car leave the parking area. Hoyt lingered in the parking area while we joined thousands of others going in the stadium.

The Florida student section was behind the Fighting Gator Band with Florida's cheerleaders in their white shirts and slacks down in the front. The football squads were on the field going through warm-up drills.

Students and friends were chattering with one another and shouting greetings. An air of excitement permeated the crowd in anticipation of the opening of the long-awaited football season. Family members of students came into and around the student sections. We saw a few people from Fort Capron and Vero.

The teams left the field to go back to their locker rooms in preparation for the opening kickoff. The band, after assembling at one end of the field, marched out playing "Cheer for the Orange and Blue." At the center of the field, the band stopped, and, at the presenting of the colors, played "The Star Spangled Banner" while the crowd stood and sang the national anthem.

As the band marched off and the teams came back onto the field, we saw Roger Hoyt climbing up the aisle next to ours by himself. He recognized us and, seemingly nervous, stopped to greet us, somewhat surprised to see Sally. He didn't know that she was going to college in Florida. It was no surprise to me that he was in Gainesville. He always went to the Florida-Stetson games. If he had a Levy County connection, this would be a good cover for making a contact. Hoyt went on up to his seat in a Stetson section several rows behind us.

Stetson won the coin toss and chose to receive. Florida boomed the kickoff to the goal line where Stetson fooled Florida with a hand-off on the return, taking the ball all the way to Florida's forty-eight yard line before the ball-carrier was stopped with a touchdown-saving tackle. That play was followed by an off-tackle slant that gained a first down for Stetson. It was obvious that the Stetson team had come to win an upset victory. Stetson did score in the second quarter and the first half ended with Florida trailing by seven to nothing.

We had arranged to meet Eddie between the halves so he could see Sally. After they greeted one another, I hastily said to Eddie, "Roger Hoyt is here by himself, and we saw him receive what looked like a payment from someone from Georgia. I have a hunch that he plans to meet someone else, maybe McCurry. I've always heard that in a criminal investigation, you should keep an eye on the suspect. Sally and I could follow him but it would be too obvious. You could do it better."

"Okay. I have Nelly parked close by in the employee's section. After the game I'll see where he goes and report back by calling you at Piggy Park. You wanted to take Sally over there, anyway, to meet Maude and Annie."

"That's perfect. We won't leave there until we hear from you."

In the locker room, Coach Bachman must have given the Gators a much needed inspirational talk because they were a different team in the third quarter. Gator fans came alive as their team marched down the field for a tying touchdown and extra point. Still, the smaller Stetson team fought diligently, holding off thrust after thrust.

Only three minutes remained in the game when Florida started its final drive. Everyone was on their feet screaming and yelling. Florida moved ever closer to the Stetson goal line, the heavier backs pounding first to the right and then to the left. Less than a minute remained when, with Florida on Stetson's three yard line, a loud yell came from behind Sally and me.

"Hold that line!" the voice shouted.

Sally and I looked at each other. We had heard that yell before. Turning around, we saw Roger Hoyt and there was no doubt in our minds about his being on the beach at Manatee Creek the night of the murder. When Hoyt saw us staring at him, a look of fright crossed his face.

Florida scored and won the hard-fought game. Roger Hoyt left his seat and made his way down the aisle as fast as the crowd would let him. Eddie was at the bottom of the next aisle over, all set to pick up Hoyt's trail. In a few minutes we saw Eddie in Nelly following behind Hoyt leaving the stadium lot in his Lincoln.

CHAPTER 20

Amid the pandemonium on the campus after Florida's narrow victory, Sally and I drove in my car to Piggy Park. Being among the first postgame customers to arrive, we were individually welcomed by Maude.

"You must be Sally," she said. "My, have we heard a lot about you, and I must say that Scotty wasn't exaggerating."

"I guess that's a compliment, for which I thank you," Sally replied. "From what I hear, you and Annie have been a big help to Scott and Eddie. They treasure your friendship."

"Where is Eddie?" asked Annie, who had come from the other end of the counter to join the greeting.

"He's checking out something for us," I said. "We asked him to give us a call here; we're going to be hanging around for a while. I hope you don't mind."

"Of course not," Maude said, "Make yourself comfortable at the stools down there by the telephone and we'll bring you whatever you want, if we got it. Gracious, it's good to meet you, Sally."

We did what Maude said as she and Annie got busy serving the crowd that began to gather from the game. Annie brought us each a hamburger and milk shake. It was good to have something to do while we anxiously waited to hear from

Eddie. An hour had passed since we saw him leaving the stadium after Hoyt in a long line of cars. The phone had rung a few times, but it wasn't Eddie. Eventually, the call came from him.

"I'm at Aunt Ellen's," he said. "I followed Hoyt out through Archer to Bronson where he stopped at a phone booth. He obviously called someone from there. He continued on through Otter Creek and kept going toward Cedar Key. I could keep up with him during the heavy traffic, but by the time I got to Otter Creek, that Lincoln was going too fast for Nelly. I remembered Aunt Ellen and she let me use her phone. What do you want me to do?"

"There's no place he could be headed except Cedar Key. There's only one way in and one way out. Go on out there and wait for me at the store. Don't try to do anything on your own. If you pass him coming back, wait for me at Aunt Ellen's. I'll see Nelly parked out in front. I'll bet he has set up a meeting with somebody. We'll decide what to do when I get there. Keep up the good work. Can you hear me all right in this noise?"

"Yes, I understood you. I'll see you later," Eddie said and hung up.

Sally, in trying to shield me from the noise in the diner, was standing close and got the gist of the conversation.

"You stay here with Maude and Annie. I'm going to Cedar Key to meet Eddie."

"There you go again!" she said, obviously peeved. "You know you're not going out there without me. Now let's get in the car and say no more about it."

I got the message and knew that there was no use arguing with her. Before leaving I told Maude that we were going to Cedar Key. She was puzzled, but I didn't explain.

"This has something to do with that murder you kids were involved in, doesn't it?" Maude said. "You be careful."

The traffic was thinning out and night was falling as we left Gainesville on the Archer road. We stopped briefly at Aunt Ellen's so she could meet Sally and I could use the telephone. Aunt Ellen could sense some excitement and was enjoying herself.

"Haven't I seen you somewhere before?" she asked Sally. "I don't think so," she replied. "I've never been around here before." She must have seen Sally's picture in the Gainesville Sun.

While they were getting acquainted, I went in another room and placed a call to Sheriff Bogart. He was usually in his office on Saturday night, which was the night when he was most likely to be needed. In fact, he answered the telephone.

"Sheriff Bogart, this is Scott Forrester. I've got to make this quick. Sally and I are in a little place west of Gainesville called Otter Creek. We're certain that Roger Hoyt is the local man that you're looking for, and that he was on that beach at Manatee Creek. He was at the Stetson game today and we recognized his voice when he shouted."

"Are you sure?" he asked, "That just doesn't seem possible."

"Certainly we're sure. We even saw him receive what we think was a payment for booze that was smuggled through that Atlanta market. He left after the game for Cedar Key, where he is probably meeting the man from Levy County that you told us to be on the lookout for. Eddie Russell trailed him and is waiting at a store out there, and Sally and I are on the way. I know you are going to tell me to wait for help but we'll be careful. Unless you have some information I need to know, I must hang up."

"Hank Slade went up to Gainesville to see the game and nose around himself. I'll call him and let him know what's going on. Don't take any foolish chances."

"We won't, but I think we better act now," I said and hung up. Aunt Ellen didn't ask any questions but said to call her if she could help. We thanked her, got in my car, and headed for Cedar Key. Eddie was waiting in the store when we got there. Roger Hoyt's Lincoln was parked at the pier.

"He's out on the houseboat. I saw the man that runs the place give him a key when I parked Nelly out back," Eddie told us when we joined him in a booth.

We could talk and move about freely because the supper customers had left and hardly anyone was around. The lights of a car coming across the bridge shone in the window. When it passed the store and parked at the pier, we could see that it was Joe McCurry's Cadillac. McCurry got out of the car and walked to the houseboat.

"Stay here with Sally. I'm going to sneak down there and try to eavesdrop on the conversation," I said.

The night was dark and the only lights were the ones coming from the open windows. Close to the houseboat was a dock box I hid behind. I could easily hear them talking.

"I must say it didn't please me none to get that telephone call from you. Bein' the front man for Cochrane in the Panhandle made sense because, sooner or later, somebody from south Florida is goin' to be elected governor, and he seemed like someone who could get elected and would do what I told him to do. But you boys sure made a mess of things down there," McCurry said. "I wasn't particular about how you get your money, but murder ain't down my line."

"That's my problem, Joe," Roger replied. "I must have your help. Until now it wasn't known, but things are closing in on me. I was on the beach helping Paul when he slugged that Bahamian with a heavy lead weight. The fool was trying to blackmail us. I helped Paul dispose of the body. They are going to pick me up for murder. They might even electrocute

me—if not, they'll send me to jail for a long time. I just could-
n't stand it. I've got to get out of the country."

"Why didn't Cochrane blow the whistle on you? He
implicated others down there."

"I threatened to hurt his wife and kids if he did. I was desperate."

"Well, what do you want me to do about it, except turn
you in?"

"You can't do that, Joe. I've got ten thousand dollars on
me and it's yours if you'll run me over to the Yucatan
Peninsula in your boat. Come on, Joe, Yucatan's not very far
across the Gulf from here. Fast as that boat is, you could be
back Monday morning, ten grand richer and you can have the
Lincoln too."

"You're crazy, Hoyt. Ain't no amount of money goin' to
get me mixed up in murder."

"What am I going to do? Those kids were at the game,
and somehow I know that they know." There was a pause,
then Hoyt continued, "I'm thirsty. Can I have a glass of water,
please?"

I had moved from my place behind the dock box, and as
I looked in the window I saw Hoyt pistol-whip McCurry
behind the ear when McCurry turned to get Hoyt some water.
McCurry dropped like a rock. Hoyt went through some keys
on a key-rack and found the one he was looking for. I ducked
behind the dock box as Hoyt left the houseboat and went
aboard McClurry's Sportsfisherman. He acted as if he had
been aboard before, easily finding the ignition switch. The
first engine started in a deep roar, followed by the second of
the powerful twin diesel engines. Hoyt moved fore and aft,
casting off the dock lines, and eased out into Waccassasa Bay.

Eddie and Sally came hurrying down the pier where I was
now standing. "What's going on?" Eddie asked.

"Plenty," I said. "McCurry is hurt and Hoyt is getting away." They followed me into the houseboat where McCurry had regained consciousness and was trying to get to his feet. We got him up and Sally found a towel, wet it, and pressed it against the egg-like bruise swelling on the side of McCurry's head.

"What happened?" McCurry asked.

"Hoyt knocked you out, took your boat, and headed for Mexico," I said.

Joe McCurry said, "We keep the fuel tanks topped off, so he could make it unless he's stopped. However, he may know how to run the boat, but he doesn't know these waters. It may be that he won't get very far. If he goes southwest in the general direction of Yucatan without following a channel through the bay, he'll pile up on a coral shelf about two miles offshore and wreck the boat."

"What can we do?" I asked.

"You can go after him in my ChrisCraft runabout and overtake him if the seas aren't rough. I can't go with you; my head is splitting so that I can't see straight. The ignition key is in that drawer."

I got in the ChrisCraft with Sally right behind me. It was useless to insist that she stay on the pier with Eddie.

"You go to the store and call for help," I yelled to Eddie as we left at high speed with the throttle all the way forward.

"How are you going to find him in the dark?" Sally hollered over the roar of the engine.

"We better hope that he runs up on that coral shelf."

Slowing down, I found the switch to a bright spotlight mounted on the bow of the ChrisCraft and shined it from side to side. As McCurry had predicted, the Sportsfisherman appeared in the gleam of the spotlight high up on the shoal. The engine was stalled and Hoyt could be seen thrashing around in the shallow water trying to push the boat off the shelf.

"We better watch it," I said to Sally. "He hit McCurry with a gun. He must have it with him. You get down."

"Hoyt! Give up," I yelled. "You're not going anywhere."

"Come and get me," Hoyt called back, firing a shot in the air.

"Have it your way. We'll just leave you out here," I said as we turned and headed for shore.

"No!" Hoyt screamed. "Don't leave me!"

We turned back toward Hoyt. "Let me see you throw that gun away."

"See, I'm doing, it," Hoyt said, and with the light turned on him, he threw the gun out into the water.

I eased the ChrisCraft over to the Sportsfisherman with Hoyt now in it. Hoyt clambered into our boat and threw himself on the backseat, pleading with me not to hurt him. With Sally handling the ChrisCraft, I tied Hoyt up with the stern lines and we headed back to Cedar Key.

McCurry was waiting for us as we pulled up to the pier. I told him that his boat was wrecked on the coral shelf just as he had expected. McCurry got aboard and went through Hoyt's jacket and removed the envelope.

"I'll take this ten thousand dollars. It'll about pay for the damage you did to my boat."

"You can't do that. It's all the money I got," Hoyt wailed.

"You ain't gonna need any money where you're goin'."

Eddie came down the pier from the store and with him was Hank Slade. Hank took Roger Hoyt in custody for transfer back to San Lucia County. Roger complained to Hank about McCurry taking his money. McCurry said Roger was just making that up.

I really liked the way Sally clung to me as we walked to

the cars. She said, "Now, maybe we can count on having a nice quiet date sometime. You've provided me with about all the adventure I need for a while. By the way, we're not out of trouble yet. You were supposed to get me back to Rollins by ten tonight. We didn't make it."

"By golly, you're right. We will stop at Aunt Ellen's and call somebody and explain. We'd better call your mother also. This is bound to be in the paper tomorrow."

Joe McCurry thanked us for the help, assuring us that if we ever needed anything in north Florida he was the man to see. By my experience this summer, I have decided with politicians, the bad guys are not as bad as we think they are, and the good guys are not as good as we think they are.

The lights were on at Aunt Ellen's. She said excitedly, "I haven't seen this much traffic going out to Cedar Key in a long spell. You all just come on in here and tell me what this is all about."

Sally and Aunt Ellen were deep in conversation as I began the telephone calls to Rollins and Sally's mother.

Epilogue

The first weekend in December

Paul Cochrane was now in the Palm Beach County jail awaiting his murder trial, which has been transferred after a motion for change of venue on the grounds that he couldn't get a fair trial in San Lucia County. Roger Hoyt was in the Florida penitentiary at Raiford serving a ten-year sentence after pleading guilty to accessory to murder and smuggling whiskey. Joe McCurry had turned in the ten thousand dollars, since it was legal evidence.

Eddie Russell has been elected president of the freshman class by the many friends he has made picking up laundry and dry cleaning in the dormitories and swamps. His Model-T was a familiar sight around the campus with its roof-top sign, "VOTE RIGHT - VOTE RUSSELL." I have been selected for a minor position on the staff of the campus weekly, "Florida Alligator." Charles Graham was doing well academically and has made the track team at Davidson.

It was the weekend of Fall Frolics at the university celebrating the end of another successful season for the Florida Gator football team. Our dates, Nell Stone and Sally Graham, were with Eddie and me walking toward the gymnasium where Glen Gray and his Casa Loma Orchestra were playing for the annual Fall Ball. We heard the music begin with the band's theme song, "Smoke Rings."

I said to Sally, "The editor of the Alligator has asked me

to do a story on the bats in an abandoned fertilizer factory on the outskirts of Gainesville. Tonight, after the ball, let's go out there and bag some bats. That will make a good story."

"Scott, you must be joking. But why would I think this date with you would be any more normal than the other ones?" was Sally's laughing reply.

THE END